TRANSITIONS

TRANSITIONS

by

Maria Herron

ISBN: 978-1-7362419-0-5 (paperback)

CHAPTER 1

Beep! Beep! Beep! The shrill cry pierced through the air like a needle popping a balloon. Only the balloon was a beautiful dream of a raven-haired, chiseled Greek god who only had eyes for me amid a sea of beach-bodied femme fatales. I was fawning over his rippling muscles as he gently caressed me until the illusion was burst by the sharp and sudden awakening to reality. First with the abrupt pop of the beeping alarm. Then the radio.

"Good Morning! This is Sam and Bob in the a.m., wishing you all a fantastic, bright, and beautiful Monday morn—" said the perky, clearly well-caffeinated radio jockey, with his upbeat tone and hyperactive, borderline-adult-ADHD level of distracted speed talking cut short by his fellow DJ, now at a momentary loss for words.

"Uh, Sam? Sam? Sam? *Sam!*" came the baritone, gruff voice of his counterpart, who was usually able to keep up with Sam's enthusiasm at half the decibel level and more clarity and was most certainly not in the mood this morning.

Sighing before composing himself enough to respond, knowing what was likely in store for him this morning, he said, "Yes, Bob?"

"It's twenty-three degrees outside."

With sarcasm, and while becoming increasingly aware of the fact they were live on the radio, Sam said, "I know it is, Bob; what's your point?"

"My point is that it is twenty-three degrees outside, and this is the warmest it has been in four weeks. It has been freezing and snowing and freezing and snowing and freezing, and have I mentioned dark yet? Oh, yeah, dark and cold and freezing and—"

"*All right,* all right! We all get it. The weather has been crap for a while now. But it shouldn't put a stop to a bright new week for our listeners, now should it?"

"There's supposed to be freezing rain after we get three more inches of snow tonight—"

With frustration straining his voice, Sam said, "Fine. You win. Here's some Metallica. 'Enter Sandman,' for all of you that should have hit the snooze one more time…"

"Well, isn't this a peachy start to another great, wintry week?" I groaned as I rolled over and did exactly what the radio jockey had told me to do. "Hit the snooze? Don't mind if I do."

At exactly a quarter to eight, the infernal beeping was at it again, and this time it meant business. It was just the kick in the pants I needed to get my ass up, I was about to be late to my very favorite place to be on a Monday morning, or any morning for that matter—*work*!

At forty-three I thought I would be much further along in my life. Granted, I do have a steady job, nice home, and adoring cat named Kiki, but I did not have much of what most would call a social life. I chose the route of work—"career," some would call it, though this was not necessarily my choice of words as I had in a short while grown to hate my job and more so my coworkers.

Groaning with disgust, "*Crap!* I knew I should have gotten up last time! Now I only have twenty minutes to get out the door. Let's go, cat! Mama's got no time to lose!" speaking to Kiki as if she were my child as I darted around the bedroom while stripping out of my pajamas and frantically searching for my glasses. "Where did I put those damn things? Note to self, make a spot on the nightstand to keep glasses right by the lamp where I can easily grab them and go because this is getting old."

As I finally slowed down to take a breath, I found my glasses in exactly the spot I wanted them to be. Now naked and not blind, I bolted into the bathroom to run through my morning routine.

"Time enough to pee, half-ass brush teeth, get dressed, feed the cat, and go."

This wasn't exactly what you would call an atypical morning. This was usually how it went. Get up late, rush around, do what I needed to just to get those few extra minutes of much-needed sleep. But I always managed to have time to critique myself in the mirror.

"If I suck this in all day, maybe it will disappear? What do you think, Kiki? The mirror always adds ten pounds, right? Or was that cameras? I can never remember," I said aloud as I tried to rub the wrinkles out of my cardigan. Always seeing myself as average in every way, I never gave myself much mind in terms of fashion or makeup. Bargain sweaters and last year's shoes gave me room to follow my passion, helping others. In the cold, cruel world, someone had to care, and it might as well be me—a motto I lived my life by.

In my mind the people who had time enough to fuss with the latest fashion trends and makeup or hair trends were better off spending half that time and energy making this world a better and more hospitable place, if that was ever even an achievable possibility (clearly not one in my lifetime, but I had to try). Taking another look in the mirror, I saw what I always knew to be the cold, hard truth; I saw her mousy, flat brown hair, like everyone else's. My pear-shaped figure, like everyone else's. My average height, like everyone else's. I could disappear into a crowd without even trying. My only saving grace, was her bright green eyes. They sparkled when I smiled, and my smile could light up a room—or so I have been told.

With a groggy, blank stare, the cat cocked her head to the side and meowed.

"You're right—not going to happen. Plan B, lose the cardigan, it is! Off I go, baby girl. Love you. See you after work."

Having always prided myself on being punctual and reliable, I was out the door within twenty minutes. Taking my dependable car on my usual route to work, I had calculated that even in bad weather—and that winter had been unseasonably bad—I would be able to make it to work in twenty-five minutes, tops. That gave me another ten minutes of buffer.

Now on the road, I continued my usual morning routine. "Dressed, check. Files, check. Coffee, check. And cell phone…" I fumbled around in my mess of a purse. "Cell phone…cell phone? Where are you, damn cell phone? *Fuck a duck!* I left it at home again! *God,* the Millennials are going to rag on me all day for that one; they don't know how to take a piss without their phones. Stupid Mondays!" I fumed.

As I irritably progressed in my drive to work, I noticed something odd in the distance on the side of the road— a car with its blinkers flashing. Strange enough to see any cars on side roads as I used them to avoid the morning traffic jam and entitled drivers; my commute would take half the time if I were willing to go to work via that congested mess. While slowly approaching, I could start to make out the image of two men acting frantic out in the bitter cold and wind with what looked like a little boy bobbing around in the back seat of the car. I slowed down to better survey whether they needed help or not. While I chanted in my head, *Please be ok, please be ok, please be ok,* one of the men, with relief written across his face, flagged me down. Reluctantly I pulled over to try and help, doing so against my own best judgment; something about this setting seemed off. I felt uneasy getting out the car; knowing the risks, I still decided to help. After all, the child in the back seat rolling around had lulled me into a false sense of safety and tugged at my heartstrings. I didn't want to leave them stranded on the side of the road in the bitter cold knowing no one else would be around to help them. I pulled over slowly, using my hazard lights so as not to be hit by any stray, gawking cars. None were expected, but that would be my luck! I bundled up tight. Yeah, it was warmer than it had been in a while, but it was still below freezing, and the wind blew right through me.

With a deep breath, I walked up with a reassuring smile on my face to meet the two men. They smiled back and seemed cordial as all three looked under the hood. They were younger than I expected—two young men with their even younger "baby brother," perhaps? The little boy stayed put in the back seat, presumably trying to keep warm; he was bundled up pretty tightly. Determined I could not help them any further without my car kit; it had all the essentials in case of emergency—tire gauge, flares, jumper cables, the works. All courtesy of my loving and slightly overprotective father, a gift given a few years before he passed away. This was his way of always looking out for me, even after he was gone. With all our heads under the hood jiggling everything that could possibly be loose, we unanimously decided to try to give it a jump start. I started toward my car, grabbing my coat tightly braving the sharp wind, when I felt a swift jerk backward, making me lose my footing, then a flash of bright white light and a floating sensation, followed by stillness.

CHAPTER 2

"Excuse me. Excuse me, Miss!"
This was all I could hear over and over again when I came to my senses. As far as vision was concerned, all I could see was white—white on white, with this warming iridescence. And this tiny voice was sounding off in the distance. "Excuse me, Miss? Can you hear me, Miss?"

I was starting to make out the image beckoning me incessantly—a woman dressed in all white from head to toe. She was tall and slender, and her hair was tucked back under a small hat, almost like one of those old-school flight attendants that you would see from back in the 1950s or 1960s. Her hair was something utterly fascinating. It seemed to be made of pure light, so bright it was blinding, yet you could not look away. Everything about her was soothing, from her voice to her gentle tone and demeanor. She persisted. "Excuse me, Miss? Are you all right?" All I could do was stare while my eyes adjusted to the copious amounts of light;

none of this—the light, the woman, the stillness—made sense.

"Honey, take your time; when you are ready, I will be here for you." The sweetness from her voice trailed away to give me some room to breathe. It was as if I were a newborn fawn struggling to get my footing. I was unable to tell which way was up—was I standing, or sitting, or lying down? The infinite amount of light surrounding me, with no furniture or seams to differentiate where the floor ended and the walls began, took a once calming white warmth and turned it into something frightening. Like a pilot flying in the fog, or a disoriented diver in the dark depths of the ocean. Unable to convince herself of anything with more than a 30 percent certainty, I began to blurt out whatever came into my once severely wounded and still throbbing head.

"Where am I? How did I get here? I thought I was on my way into the office...am I at the hospital? Where are the doctors? Are you a nurse? Why is your hair so bright?" It took this burst of questions to give me the momentum to sit upright and the motivation to move more than a few inches. Enough to feel around the smooth and warm surroundings. With only the woman there to base any depth perception on, I surmised that i was sitting on the floor, only to crane my neck upward to gaze at the already incredibly tall woman. With only a slight hesitation, I began to bring myself to my knees and then, with much more ease than I anticipated, to my feet.

Standing up, I began to realize how effortless it was

to move. This was new; I had always felt as if I had pre-maturely aged. Old, rickety bones.

Now to test walking, I thought. *One foot in front of the other, nice and slow.* As my feet caught up with my brain, I realized everything was perfectly fine. I began to walk around and examine the room; it still looked as if there wasn't a wall in sight. It was so odd. It was pure white, but you couldn't tell where it was coming from; there wasn't a light source anywhere. It was just bright. I looked down at the floor, and that is when I thought, *Umm, these aren't my clothes.* From my shirt to my pants to my shoes, I was dressed in all white myself. "What the crap is this?" Well, of course I had to check, and even the underwear and bra were white! "Seriously? How? I hope he was cute." As I laughed to myself, I circled around and realized something was missing. The bench I had been sitting on was now gone. I kookily did a full circle to see where it had gone, and I was truly alone. Nothing, as far as my eyes could see.

"Where did the girl go?" I said out loud. The room didn't echo, as if the light absorbed the sound. "Ok, let's see where I am. I was headed to work and woke up on a bench. So I am not at work, and now I can't find the bench. Peachy. Just peachy..." I couldn't help but be sarcastic; it was ingrained in my personality and partially a defense mechanism I had developed over the years.

"Miss, I believe you were looking for me?" said the sweet, soothing voice, which scared me out of my last remaining wit; it startled me to the point that I yelped and became airborne from fright. I reminded myself of those old cartoons where the dog scares the cat, and it winds up on the ceiling. If only I could find the ceiling in this case!

As I whipped around to see who and where it was coming from, I saw the lady from before. I didn't recognize her as much by looks as by the vague, blurry outline and glowing hair. Now that she was in focus, I could see how truly striking she was. Tall and slender, as I could tell originally. But now I could get a good look at her face. I had never seen anyone so beautiful. So simple and yet so radiant—skin flawless, like a porcelain doll I had as a kid. Bright blue, almond-shaped eyes beneath long black eyelashes, with perfectly pink lips. This woman put Barbie to shame, especially with her hair, so golden it glowed.

"Umm, I was just wondering where I was. I thought I was on my way to work. Am I at the hospital or something? I know they said it was new and state of the art, but where are the beds?"

Giggling, she said, "Oh no, dear. You are not at a hospital at all. You will have no need for such things here. You have made it to the gates. I am your escort; my name is Petra. I know you are in shock, and we will help you every step of your way."

My stomach dropped to my knees. "Gates! What gates? Are you trying to tell me I am d...de..." I came crashing into the realization I was not at all where I had thought I was.

"Oh, dear! Have a seat."

Just then the bench reappeared behind me. She helped me sit down since I nearly missed trying to do so myself and sat with me while holding my hand and comforting me. "I know this is a trying time, and this is all so new and shocking to you, but you will be ok. I promise."

In a state of shock, I said, "This isn't right…" I could not stop muttering to myself how wrong this felt. "I'm not old enough to die, I'm not ready to die, and I still haven't even gotten married! Lord knows I've tried! I have so much left to do; I still had all my saved-up vacation days, which I will never be able to cash in on! My family! Oh, God! My poor mother and sister! Do they know? How long have I been gone! My cat! Oh no! Please tell me she is ok; she is my baby! Is she ok? Are they all ok?" I begged her.

"Relax, dear, relax. All in due time. Your family knows, and your cat is safe—feisty one, from what I am told. They will heal; now it is time for you to heal. Now take a few deep breaths and relax your mind. One thing at a time; try not to overwhelm yourself."

As I followed her instructions and tried to clear my head, I found it harder and harder to push all the questions out. My heart raced, and my eyes darted with every thought. First off, if I am at the gates, where are the gates? Where is the judgment? Is this where she tells me I was not good enough to get into heaven and a trapdoor opens up and I free-fall screaming down to hell? I definitely was panicking, and based on her facial expression, I think she could sense it.

"I know you have many, many questions, and you will have every last one answered when you are ready, but let me help you understand what is happening. Now, I know this is all so confusing to you."

I thought she could read it off my face, but was she reading my mind? *Let's test; I'm thinking of a number between one and ten.*

"Everything looks so new and different from what you are used to." She paused and looked directly into my eyes. "Seven?" she said surely and then continued, which scared me away from having any other stray thoughts. "But we are all here to help you transition; this will be your home from now on. You will have a caretaker; he or she will look after you for as long as you need them around."

After a few deep breaths, I managed, "A caretaker? Like a nanny? Is that necessary?" I tried to suppress my thoughts, even the most basic. I found it too creepy that she knew my every thought. *I wonder if everyone here is like that.*

"Darling, your caretaker will come in handier than you realize; he or she will appear once you are settled into your new home. When you are ready, we can go right through here; I will be happy to show you the way. Oh, other than me, they will be the only ones openly able to know your thoughts. They do this only to help you develop; nothing to fret about, dear."

As she said that, a door appeared, much like the

bench had disappeared and reappeared only when needed. The door was as tall as my eyes could see; a seam split open more than a regular hinged door but stretched infinitely. Slowly light began to seep in—not the same stark, clean, bright, vibrant light that surrounded us, but a warming, yellow light, one that filled your heart and soul with the soothing sweetness of a hot drink on a long, cold winter day. Like a curious and frightened child, I clasped her arm as she led me; we walked carefully through the threshold. As if it were magic, I no longer had fear; the light was warm and invited me in like an old friend's open arms welcoming my embrace.

The other side was magnificent. Everything I thought it would be and yet so much more. So light and warm—and the best part, so safe! As if the weight of the world was off my shoulders, making me feel light as a feather. And I could finally breathe! I could finally be at ease and live—umm, well—yeah, you know what I mean.

"Do you like what you see?" Petra asked me as she read my mind—umm, about that one too.

"This is so beautiful" was all I could muster. From the moment we stepped through, I could only see and smell happiness—that's right, *smell* happiness. Everything I loved from my life: large open meadows full of wildflowers that smelled of a clean, crisp breeze. It even had a hint of freshly mowed grass. There were small animals scurrying around, chasing each other; off in the distance, there were snowcapped mountains with waterfalls etched into their sides. Ruins lay between the trees, ruins much older than any I had ever seen, even in books or on TV. The further down the path we walked, the more beautiful it was. There was only one house in sight, a small cottage. Warm and cozy, with a wisp of smoke coming out of its chimney, something straight out of a Thomas Kinkade painting.

"That is for you," she said.

"I can't even believe it; is this really happening? That is my house? I have always wanted one; I never in my entire life thought I would be able to have that." This is when I realized, *Duh, dead, silly rabbit.* "So let me get this straight—this is heaven? Where are the cherubs and the clouds to lounge on?"

With a laugh, she said, "Oh no, dear; heaven is not like that. I do not know where people started to get that crazy idea from, but it is simply not true. Heaven is what you make it. It is different for every person. It is what you feel you deserve and includes everything you love or want to have."

"Everything I love? But where is my family?" I asked as we approached the door to my cottage.

"Your family will come in time; all in time. When you are ready, you will be able to see and experience much more than even this. Now follow me in, and I will show you around."

We stepped through the threshold, and I instantly felt warm and cozy all over. It smelled of sweet cinnamon and a log fireplace. The cottage was wooden, and it had exposed beams running the length of the house and a wooden, slatted vaulted ceiling. As I stumbled through what felt like a drunken stupor fueled by overwhelming joy, my eyes could only take in so much; they welled with tears. Every way I turned, I was awed by something I had always wished to have or something I had always loved, like the fresh-cut lilies on a knitted tablecloth on the dining room table. Bookshelves full of old books, and the ladder! How I had always wanted one of those ladders that rolled between the shelves! The color on the walls—soothing cream, one with burgundy accents. Even the floors were perfect. Everything was perfect. Tears began rolling down my cheeks in steady streams. Every time I wiped them away, more replaced them instantly.

"May I see my bedroom?" I shakily asked.

"Right this way, honey," she said as she led me by my arm into the bedroom, being as compassionate and understanding as anyone could be. She slowed herself to a snail's pace so that I could take it all in without becoming overwhelmed.

We walked into even more beauty. A fireplace roaring with fire and a bed beautifully dressed with all the bells and whistles. A plush down comforter at least four inches thick—I had never seen one so fluffy. And the bed adorned with rows upon rows of neatly arranged pillows.

"Lace," I mumbled. "It even has lace…" As I trailed off into unconsciousness, I could feel Petra helping me into my new bed. It felt like a warm glove on a cold day and instantly made me relaxed, the kind of Zen you get on those lazy Saturday mornings where you don't need to rush around anywhere and sit in pajamas all day just because you can.

"Before you fall asleep, my dear, I have to remind you, your caretaker will be here tomorrow for you. He or she will appear when needed and will help you. Now rest peacefully, darling; your journey has been long and challenging." At least I thought she said "challenging"—the last bit got a little dicey. As my head hit the pillows, I floated into a dreamless sleep.

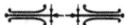

Rolling over the next morning, I could still hardly believe it. I had slept like a rock, which was so strange since all my life I had always been a light sleeper. Slowly I looked around the room and scrutinized every inch. There were paintings on the walls of exquisitely detailed nature scenes; the trees looked so lifelike you could see the breeze flow through the branches. The bed and furniture all in mahogany, matched and seemingly handmade. The mattress, so soft, cradled my tushy. I could have rolled around in it all day! There weren't any knickknacks around, which was how I liked it—less to dust and less clutter. The fire was still lit in the fireplace, emitting a warm glow; it hadn't gone out overnight, making me wonder if it was even real. *The logs next to it look real. Hmm. Do I really want to get out of bed and check? What about that door on the left? Is that a closet? A bathroom? Heaven needs a bathroom? That just sounds gross,* I mused to myself. *Where would heavenly poop*

flow? Ha! So, of course, curiosity got the best of me, and up I was out of bed.

No pain! What? It had been at least ten years since I had been able to freely hop out of bed without a moan, groan, crack, or pull! This was *fantastic*! I didn't know what excited me more—the thrill of adventure or the excitement stirred from not needing to hobble around for ten minutes after I got out of bed before looking like a human and not Igor from that *Frankenstein* movie.

It took a few minutes to get over the excitement. It also took a couple of stretches and more than a few victory laps around the bed. I just needed to make sure it wasn't some short-term euphoric side effect of my transition. After I regained my wits, I decided to explore the exit on stage left, the mystery door. As I stood directly in front of it, I thought of all the things it could be—well, only two practical rooms came to mind, really, but it was still fun to think I could have a crafts nook or a zoo attached to my bedroom. A girl can dream, right? I swung open the door to reveal…

A walk-in closet. Exciting, but not too much so. It still was enough to cause a little drool, but not a puddle. I started to get my hopes up for a zoo with a tiger or two. I have always loved tigers—so pretty. My mind trailed off on a tangent (pretty standard stuff, actually).

I mindlessly walked into the closet and flipped on the light switch. The layout and the clothes were almost identical to what I had left behind. "That's strange—no fancy, I-can-have-anything-I've-ever-wanted clothes? I get the house but not the wardrobe of the stars, I guess."

Thumbing through the rack, I could see some of my favorites, but they were not as worn as I had left them, as if they had been revived to be like new. I turned off the light and closed the door behind me as I left the rather deflated scene of the closet. As I stood in the bedroom, I thought, *But don't I need a bathroom?* Just as I thought this up, I realized I had missed a door on the right of the bed.

Ah, exit stage right! I said to myself and waltzed over to the door, swung it open without any delay, and found the master bathroom. "Now this is what I am talking about!" I said out of amazement. For every charming detail the bedroom contained, the bathroom had one too, but with much more flair. Double sink with a full-length counter crowned by a full-length mirror and all the cabinet space a girl could possibly need. It was marble from top to bottom, chrome finishes accenting the opulence and elegance; nothing quaint about this room, not in the slightest. The shower had the jets on the sides and one of those showerheads that was like a waterfall—whatever those were called. I was too excited to even try to remember. It was large, too—not too large, though, just perfect to sing and dance in but not feel like you could bathe an entire sports team in! Everything appeared untouched and unused; even the toilet appeared immaculate. I stared in awe for at least ten more minutes and then decided it was time to move on to the next room. This was, of course, after I had opened every cabinet and drawer to inspect the contents. To my greatest delight, it had all my must-haves in life—my hair products, my skin products, even the manicure set I could not live without! No pun intended, of course! Though I would never, by any stretch of the imagination, call myself vain, I did always keep myself neat and clean in appearance.

As I headed out the bedroom door, a small trinket caught my eye. It was a photograph on the nightstand, something I had previously missed. As I picked up the unique frame, a twisted metal object with ornate floral detailing, I realized just how much it stood out in a wood cabin. "How did I miss this?" I said. There were two little girls in white dresses holding balloons. The picture looked aged, almost burned around the edges. I couldn't quite place the girls; they looked familiar, yet I couldn't remember who they were. They were pretty close in age—maybe six- and eight-years-old—with blond hair, fair complexions, and light eyes. It was their eyes that looked most familiar to me, yet I still could not remember who they were. "How strange." Setting the picture down where I had found it, I decided to continue my tour and make my way back down the hall into the rest of the house.

Finally pulling myself out of the bedroom, I entered the hall—no pictures? The idea seemed odd to me, but, whatever, it was just a hall, right? Moving toward the front of the house, I passed the dining room and stopped to smell the lilies. They were stargazers, my favorite, so pungent I could smell them before I entered the room and could still smell them as I entered the kitchen off the dining room. I wandered around the kitchen as I had the bathroom. Everything I needed in its place. "This is just like the kitchen I had at home. No upgrade was required here; I *don't cook*, so why bother with *gourmet*?" I laughed to myself. I didn't bother to take notice of the intricate detail work on the cabinets, or even what was behind their beautifully crafted doors.

Now to the best part of the house—just off the entry was the living room with the mile-high bookshelves. The room was encompassed in books, the good ones, hard-cover, and most had leather binding. Volume upon volume of knowledge at my fingertips! The shelves covered all three walls; they surrounded the fireplace, leaving just enough room to avoid disaster. In this room as well, the fire was still roaring and still had the sweet smell of cinnamon; it made me wonder if the wood was infused with cinnamon or something, because the smell made me grin from ear to ear! There was also another distinct odor that made me feel right at home—the smell of the leather-bound books themselves. It was almost like a musty smell, something rather masculine yet very comforting.

I needed to see which ones I had! I did a straightaway to the ladder. "Now let's test this baby out!" I rolled it side to side first, just to make sure it was stable, and then I slowly put my weight on the first step and hoisted myself up. The shelf I was at contained classic sci-fi; it had all the greats, from Bradbury to Wells. I roamed through the titles and pulled out a few to set aside to read or, in some cases, reread. The rest of that whole unit was novels on top of novels on top of novels. I gave myself a little nudge to test the ladder's rolling capabilities. Last thing I needed to do was push too hard and fly off the ladder to the other side of the room. So a nudge to start was good enough for me. It rolled easily but not far and definitely needed more than a nudge to get anywhere. So I pushed a little harder and wobbled my way to the next shelves. "This is going to take some getting used to." This section was all history related, from prehistoric to current events—or, shall I say, the current events as I knew them.

I rolled to the last section, almost exhausted from excitement, and I only glanced through them to see what I had available to me. The Bible, as well as many other religious documents, filled this section. I couldn't believe my eyes: There were so many works I had never seen before, some so old I thought they would turn to dust if I even touched them. That's when I noticed that not all the religious works were even Christian. I saw the books for Islam, Hinduism, and Buddhism, among others. As I picked up a beautifully illustrated Bhagavad Gita and began to thumb through the incredibly old edition, I thought, *This is amazing, but why is it here?*

"Why wouldn't it be here?" said the man slamming shut the refrigerator door and chomping into an apple the size of his fist.

The shocking appearance of someone in my house scared me so much I almost fell off the ladder as I clasped my hand over my chest, with the other hand still white-knuckling the ladder, and I gave a gasping, startled scream. "Jesus Christ! Who are you?" I shouted at the stranger while I heard thunder rolling in closely, as if a storm were chasing in from the distance.

"Well, first off, don't do that; second, calm down; and third, what is this delicious fruit I am eating?"

My head was spinning; I couldn't even begin to think straight, and all I could manage was "Who?"

"Me? Oh yes, of course! Sorry, I always forget to introduce myself. Hello, my name is Gabe," he said in a curious accent as he leaned forward to shake my hand; the accent reminded me of a British one but was somehow more proper. He was tall and slender with light, sandy brown–colored hair. He had a sun-kissed glow to him, with piercing green eyes behind long eyelashes. He was wearing a white linen shirt, slightly open and loose on his skin, paired with khaki cargo pants and sandals. He reminded me of a hippie but wasn't quite one; he had the relaxed, calm demeanor but still maintained an assertive quality—like "I'm a nice guy, but you don't want to mess with me," that type of edge, which gave him an attractive quality. His handshake was firm, and he gave off the impression he was much older than he seemed. "I am your caretaker; I am here to help you through the transition," he said as he made himself comfortable on my couch. "Have a seat, and I will explain a few things to you." So, of course, I obediently sat down across from him in what felt like the softest leather chair I had ever encountered and leaned forward like the brownnosing student I was.

"To make this all easier on you, I will begin with telling you why you need a caretaker and who I am. As I said, my name is Gabe; I have been a caretaker for newcomers for centuries, far longer than I would like to admit. I know my way in and out of this land and all throughout this world. I have known many a good soul and work toward conditioning more to move on to their next lives—" His speech was so robotic I began to tune him out. It was clear he had done it for so long he now lacked in every emotion and even facial expression. Luckily I was able to catch one small phrase.

"Wait, what?" My jaw hit the floor. "Next lives?"

With a rather irritated face, as if saying, "Do *not* interrupt me," he took another bite to polish off the apple he had wolfed down and continued. "Yes, next life. This is not the end, Carol; this will be your home for however long you see fit, and then your soul moves on to your next transition. You see, there are multiple levels of heaven to go through. This is where you entered; you then move up when you feel you are ready, and after you have decided it has been long enough, you transition back to the mortal Earth. That is your permanent transition, though—that one will be the end of Carol and the beginning of a new life, a new cycle, so to speak. Your new cycle will have no recollection of its life as Carol, as you currently have none of your previous lives. This, however, is far away from where you are now." He said this so confidently and in such a rehearsed manner, as if mocking me for not already knowing this was true.

"I'm, I'm, I'm a little shocked…"

"I couldn't tell," he said in a surprisingly sarcastic tone, unexpected even for him. "Now, as I was saying, I am here to help you through this part of your journey; you can ask me any questions you need, and I come whenever truly needed. I have been assigned to you because you are a special case—not my only special case, so please keep that in mind when you need me and I am unable to come at your beck and whim." He got a little snarky at the end but checked himself and continued in a softer tone. "Special cases such as you usually require more time to become accustomed to their new surroundings, usually due to trauma, disturbances, sadness, longing, etcetera, etcetera."

"I'm sorry, how am I a special case? This house is amazing; I don't think I did anything in my time on Earth to warrant being considered a special case. Did I?"

"You are still quite new; I am telling you this to forewarn you of what is in store for your future. You will feel sadness and heartache and longing, as well as any other human emotion, until you have begun your next transition, where you will overcome these obstacles and feelings. You may not have them now, but you will later, and no, you are not a special case because of *your* actions."

"I thought heaven was supposed to be all happiness and bliss; why do I need to go through more sadness and heartache?"

"It is happiness and bliss, but like everything else, you must go through these emotions to make yourself stronger."

"I see," I said as I paused for a brief time. "I still

don't understand how I am a special case. My life was boring; what makes me so special that I get you instead of someone else? And what exactly is so special about you? Umm, no offense."

With a raised eyebrow, he said, "None taken. But to clarify, I am your caretaker because I have been around the longest; I am the most sought-after and most knowledgeable. Now, if you would like to dive right in to why you are with me, I can help you with that." His tone softened. "Carol, do you remember the day you died? What was your last memory?"

I had to think about this one. "The last thing I remember was being cold and driving to work. But that's the last thing I can think of."

"That is all you can recall? Your drive to work? Nothing out of the ordinary stands out?"

"I honestly can't remember; so much has changed in the past day I would have to think about it. That is so strange; it just happened, though. Why can't I remember it?" My mind went fuzzy with broken images of the last day. Getting dressed, then getting into the car. I remembered the cold and the gloom but not much else.

"About a month has passed technically, but it's ok, don't push yourself; you will remember in time. Let us take a look around your house, and maybe that will help clear your head and trigger memories."

"Past month…" I replayed the phrase in my head. The statement made my stomach do an involuntary back flip. I was now more confused than I had been when he first showed up, and my brain felt like a jumbled mess.

It felt like the die inside a magic eight ball after being passed around at a party. I didn't have a single coherent thought left in my head; the overload began to blur my vision and sent me stumbling. "How could it have been so long? I thought it was just yesterday," I was able to blubber out.

"Calm down." He tried to soothe me. "Calm down. Take a couple of deep breaths; no need to get worked up. It is just that time does not flow the same here as it does on Earth. In your short life, days are measured in seconds, minutes, and hours, while here it flows by events. Like water flowing in a river, it will seem, when undisturbed, as if it is standing still, when in reality there is a strong undercurrent roaring through that may never scratch the surface. We are on the surface, while life below is the undercurrent; only when you break the surface do you feel the current below. Does that make sense?"

"No!" I was still too shocked to understand a word of his little analogy.

"Ok, let me be more literal. Time does not exist here; you are only in space. This space is infinite—only when you check in on Earth will you know where you are in time. Otherwise, time does not and will not affect you here, nor should it ever have to. Does that make more sense? There is no need to keep track of time as you were used to; there are no appointments and schedules to keep. In fact, there are no clocks to measure time as you once knew it. It has been approximately a month since you have been gone."

"Yes, I think I understand." This was where I was going to have a panic attack. "*Month!* But what about my family? I didn't even get a chance to say goodbye! What about my cat! Oh, she was just a baby! How could this even happen?" The feelings and emotions and stress all came flooding back in my head. The tears welled up in my eyes, and I could not stop them from flowing. I was so upset. Upset I had forgotten about them so quickly, upset I was gone, upset I couldn't even remember how it happened, and guilty for leaving. Out of rage I started to swear until I saw the look on Gabe's face.

"This will not do," he said with a deeply concerned look on his face, and shaking his head, he gently touched my temple. The moment his fingers touched my temples, I was out like a light.

CHAPTER 3

The birds were what woke me from a deep sleep. I could hear them chirping gleefully outside of my window. The fire crackling and the soft and cozy bed could have kept me in my coma for God only knows how long, but it was as if the birds knew it had been long enough. They chirped and cooed away until my eyes were wide open. I rolled over and stared at the picture of the two little girls until I was ready to get up. "Since time does not exist, let's call it noon." I laughed to myself.

The conversation with Gabe slowly came back to me, especially the look he had given me before he knocked me out. One month? How could that be? I got up and started toward the kitchen. I needed my coffee. Though here I did not get those caffeine headache cravings I did at home, it still was a driving force and the motivation I sorely needed to get out of bed. "I wonder how long I have been out this time? Maybe another month? Two months? A year!"

"Eh, it's been about a month, I would say," Gabe said, startling me and the coffee right out of my hands. The mug went crashing to the floor, spilling everywhere and sending shards of porcelain in every direction.

"Jesus Christ!" I shouted. "Don't do that to me! I could have had a heart attack!" The goofy look on his face when I said that, as if he were thinking, *What the heck is that?* made me chuckle. How quickly fear turned to anger and mellowed to laughter. As this happened in rolled a nasty storm, or at least it sounded like it, though the sky was oddly bright.

"What did I tell you about not saying that?"

"Saying what, heart attack?" I grinned.

"No, his name in vain. He doesn't like that. In fact, it makes him a little angry, if you haven't already noticed," he said as he pointed upward, clearly not referring to my attic.

I looked up as he pointed and, dumbfounded, stated, "So he does exist?"

"Of course he exists! His story is much older than time itself, and he is certainly not what many of your storybooks back on Earth have told you."

"Really? What is he, then?" I asked

"I hate answering this question, but if you want to know that, we will need to get comfortable. This will probably be helpful to know, anyway. Grab your coffee, and let us have a seat." He pointed to the coffee mug full of piping hot coffee, back on the counter as if it had never left my clumsy fingers and crashed to the ground. The floor, too, was spotless, as if the whole thing had never happened. Not a single remaining shard or droplet of coffee. It was shocking yet satisfying to know I didn't have to get down on hands and knees to scour the floor, only to have it still sticky for days.

"Let me see; where do I want to start…hmm. Well, I guess I should start at the beginning—my beginning, that is. I first met him when I arrived here, a very long time ago. Heaven was not as it is today; there were not as many souls to keep as of yet. He ushered me through the gates and into my home. He helped me transition through my own grief. When I was ready, he showed me my purpose and how I would help more people like me, as well as much more, shall I say, upsetting cases. He is very old and very kind. He is wisdom itself. He knows everything you would ever need to know and comes from a place that even I do not understand. He takes the form of whatever puts your mind at the most ease and you find the most comforting. I have seen him in many forms to suit the needs of many. He is known by many names and has been written about for centuries. Everyone knows he exists, but his might, grace, and infinite wisdom are beyond human comprehension. This is not to say humans are incapable of understanding, but rather that his abilities far surpass the current human capacity. This is what we believe has caused so much turmoil on Earth—humans cannot wrap their minds around a being so powerful, and so they decide to take what they believe they know about him and build their faith around their limited knowledge of his existence. No fault of their own; they just cannot comprehend the depth of his abilities."

"So you mean to tell me he is the basis of every religion on Earth?"

"Yes and no. There are quite a few obscure religions based around beliefs that do not revolve around him, but those are based on delusions of grandeur, founded in nothing other than one specific person's idea of utopia or, even worse, anarchy."

"I see," I said as I nodded along.

"As I was saying," he continued, "this world is his baby, so to speak. He has run the show since the beginning of Earth's time; he has seen everything through and has caused all the transitions that have taken place."

"Oh, so he is why the dinosaurs died?" I couldn't resist the temptation to ask.

"That is what you choose to focus on?" he asked after a long pause. "The dinosaurs?"

As I began to blush, I stumbled over my words and cleared my throat. "Sorry. As you were saying?"

"Each transition signals a new beginning—not only to humans, obviously. It is done to humans and animals alike. Each needs to move forward in ways only he can understand. This is why each and every living being on Earth is so complex. Each of those roots has gone far deeper than any of your scientists have yet to discover and is part of an even bigger picture. But not all those roots are seeded from a soul; souls are for humans and what humans have attached to."

"Attached to? What does that even mean?"

"That is a good question—finally. Humans can attach their souls to all sorts of items, including animals, clothing, or even furniture. Over my existence I have seen many things people have decided to attach their souls to, and when their existence is destroyed on Earth, those, too, will find their way back to their owner to reunite the soul."

"Really?"

"Yes, really," he stated matter-of-factly. "This is usually done out of love, the strongest bond humans are able to create. Not to be confused with the strongest emotion."

"Which is…" I couldn't resist going off on this tangent.

"Well, it is not hate. People always assume it is hate. Not sure why, either—hate is barely an emotion, more of a state of mind. Truly, the strongest emotion is fear. Love creates the strongest bond because it is shared between the two parties; fear is singular. Fear is so strong it can create its own energy. It has the ability to stop people in their tracks and drive people to do things they would under other circumstances never do. Never underestimate fear, Carol; fear, along with ignorance, will be the true downfall."

"I see" was all I really could muster; he had gone a lot darker than I had expected, which was hard to be a smartass about. Besides, how could I even imagine someone so powerful and so ancient? "So, 'souls,' you say…" As I trailed off, I gestured toward changing the subject back to his original intent.

"Yes, as I was saying—there are a finite amount of souls. These are all made by him, unique in every way, yet each and every soul is connected. Even by the tiniest thread, every human has a connection to every other human on Earth. After each soul leaves the body for its next transition, it finds its connection to the rest; this does not happen instantly, however. It is too much information to process for most and becomes overwhelming to the unwilling. This is why stages exist within heaven. I believe this is as far as we need to go today. Do you have any questions?" He stopped abruptly.

"Um, that kind of was a lot of information. I may need some time to process it all," I said.

"Take all the time in the world," he said, and before I could even blink, he was gone, just completely vanished as if he was never there. I looked around, knowing I wouldn't be able to find him, but I did it for my own sanity and definitely did not see him. "Not sure what will take me longer to process—his popping in and out or all this stuff about souls. Was I supposed to take notes?" I said out loud as I rubbed my temples, massaging the blood rushing to my brain.

"Transition, huh? I guess that sounds like a good way of explaining it." I sat there and processed for a while, and without a clock I had no idea what time it was, but I had definitely gotten hungry. So I finished my coffee, which to my astonishment never even went cold, and went into the kitchen. I opened the refrigerator to find something to snack on. Wasn't exactly sure what I was looking for, but raiding the fridge was what I did best. I opened the door, the light popped on, and what did I see? An empty refrigerator! Seriously?

"How can that even be? I saw Gabe taking an apple out of here before. Was that all that was ever in here? I am so confused. I am hungry and can't even eat?" I closed the fridge and now could not stop thinking about delicious food—some rich, creamy cheesecake, or cheesy mac and cheese. Maybe even those little frozen ice cream bars I always loved to snack on. Then I thought of those big, juicy burgers they had at the place down the street from my house. Those were amazing—thick-cut bacon on top of perfectly cooked beef with a generous helping of provolone cheese and garlic mayo. Add fresh lettuce and tomato on seasoned Texas toast—I couldn't even stand the idea, I was so hungry for it.

"This will kill me all over again, I am so hungry," I said as I opened the fridge in one last desperate plea for food. And what do I see? Just as I had imagined it, steam and all, the burger of my dreams. I whimpered as I greedily reached in, so excited yet strangely so scared that it was an illusion or a trick. I grasped the plate. The weight felt very real, so I pulled it out slowly, all in an effort to not lose a morsel, and set it on the kitchen counter. I inspected and marveled at the burger as if I had never seen one before but really was looking closely because it was too perfect.

"This is identical to the one from home; how can that be?" This was so strange, yet it looked so good. "Ah, hell, it can't kill me now, can it? Bottoms up!" I said as I grasped the burger with both hands and sunk my face nose deep into Texas toast. I tossed it around in my mouth, and every taste bud seemed to scream for more, so I did as I was told and dove in for more, and for more, and for more. It was exactly as I wanted and remembered, every last filling bite of it. When I had finished, I craved a Coke, so testing my luck, I opened the fridge, and there was the bright red can I was looking for. "Perfection!" I said as I popped the top and chugged to my heart's content. "One could get used to this for sure!" I pondered what had just happened and realized I only had what I needed or really wanted; I did not need a fridge full of food to choose from; I needed one thing to get over my hunger. "If I had only thought of doing it like that in life, I could have been a model." I laughed to myself. "But who am I kidding? I probably would have been closer to a Hungry Hungry Hippo instead. Ha!"

I dragged my butt out of the kitchen and plopped into my chair. I stared off into the fire for a bit and mulled over a few things Gabe had said, like the fact of a finite number of souls and that most religions were based around the same god but went by different names. It brought more questions to mind: "Will I ever meet him? What about these other souls? Where are they? Will I meet them?" Now I was curious how we were all connected. Last I checked, there were billions of people running around Earth, and each and every one of us were connected somehow. This was a very tough concept to believe. How was I connected to anyone from China? How was that even fathomable?

Just daydreaming and zoning out by the fire, I managed to not even notice it had turned to night on me.

This was a first for me. "Usually someone knocks me out before I can see a sunset around here." I chuckled to myself. I walked out my front door to see a sight you could only see from the *other side.* Awestruck, I could never have imagined seeing this while I was alive. The sunset here looked as if it were a mixture of the northern lights and the most romantic sunset from a Southern charm romance movie. The colors were so vivid, vibrant, and beautiful, the full color spectrum from deep, dark reds to bright yellows and cobalt blues. They swirled overhead, and when they combined, it created even more vibrant colors mixing and swirling above me like a vortex. The colors bounced and played with the light emitted from the slowly appearing stars, and as the sun went down, the swirling colors played a game of hide-and-seek with the sun's rays as it disappeared behind the horizon line. I watched the whole event from start to finish, enjoying every playful second, not even sure if I had blinked a single time; I couldn't bear missing even a moment. How could you? It was all so elegant and beautiful, like a ballet of colors dancing above your head.

I headed back indoors, careful not to run into the door from my daze, and plopped back down in my armchair. I stared up and down the bookshelves mindlessly, and that is when I realized, for the first time, *I have nowhere to go, nowhere to be, no one and nothing depending on me. I am free to do as I please, when I please, how I please.* As the thought, "What do I do now?" settled in my head, the freedom I had longed for became very real in a very dark way. I had thought on it so long it was beginning to overwhelm me. I felt it in my chest—the idea of not being needed was truly suffocating, as if the walls were closing in on me and this was not heaven at all but a deep, dark void of depression. I had spent every waking moment helping others, and the idea of not having someone else to focus on and only focusing on my own needs had me freaking out. The room kept getting darker and darker around me until I could not take it anymore and leaped out of my chair and ran out of the front door.

Trying to outrun the tunnel vision, I slammed my body into the porch rail so hard I nearly flipped over the side into the perfectly weeded and manicured roses in my front lawn. The jolt brought me back to my new, solitary reality. The scare cleared my senses and made me realize I was running from no one but myself and my own inner demons. This was heaven; this was what everyone wanted in the end, everything they wished for—to be without any worries or stress. Why was I so scared? There was no going back, only moving forward. I could now relax. I needed the crisp night air to clear my thoughts and finally convinced myself to reenter my own home. It felt like if I walked back inside, it would be a confirmation to me that this was all real and really happening, not some crazy, acid-trip-style dream. Not that I ever did anything like that; I had always been too responsible to be the party girl.

"This is my home, this is my eternity, and I will learn to love it," I repeated to myself to try and soothe my senses. With a deep breath, I pushed open the door and stood in the entry as if I had never been there before. "I love this place; I love this place," I said to myself over and over again. "Now, what do I do with myself for the rest of eternity?" I asked myself as I stared absentmindedly at the hundreds, if not thousands, of books I now owned. "Oh, duh!" I couldn't even believe I had been such a moron. I had my love right in front of me. I had even pulled out a stack to start on. I sat in my chair, bounced around to position myself comfortably for a long haul, and grabbed the first book off the stack and began to read. "Chapter 1…"

It had been a long time, even by my new standard of "time," since I had heard from Gabe. I was beginning to wonder if he had forgotten about me. I made myself entirely comfortable in my new home. Learned every nook and cranny and had a routine down. I polished off book after book and now thoroughly enjoyed my new life on a daily basis. I had read so much and felt so knowledgeable in ways I never thought I would be. I would think about how back on Earth I never would have had the time to get through the books I had gotten through here. Some I would not even have been able to touch because they were so long and complicated. Yet I could read them with ease and was able to enjoy them because I actually had time and patience enough to digest their complications and subtleties.

My routine had become a simple one: Wake up, make my bed (oddly the one thing that did not automatically clean itself up), and go get coffee, which was sitting for me on the kitchen counter, piping hot and made to perfection. Then, sit outside and watch and enjoy nature. After finishing my coffee, I would come back in and choose a new book to read. I then sat and read until I was hungry and would think of what I wanted to eat, open the fridge, grab it, gobble down my food, then back to the couch to continue to read. I would read until the book was finished, and if it was still light out, I would grab a new book and finish that before I went to bed. I started fresh every morning. It was great—so comfortable, no distractions, something I had never known in my life. The freedom that I thought would be so crippling turned out to be exactly that, freeing.

The idea never left my head—where was Gabe? He said he would be here when I needed him. The thought would drift from my mind for a while, and it would creep back in occasionally, but since I was happy, I figured he wouldn't need to come around. It's not like I remembered anything more about what he had asked me, and he didn't seem to push, so I didn't think not remembering was a big deal. I would sit there for a while and search my brain for more memories to try and fill in my own blanks. I remembered that morning and driving to work. That part was clear, but what happened after? Drifting off into my own memories, I could remember bits and pieces, like the cold, the broken-down car, the men, and the little boy. But what else? What after that?

This was still a mystery to me. Once I realized I was getting a headache from it all, I couldn't think anymore. I stood up to shake it off and decided to go inside and grab a book to read. "Maybe if I relax my mind, it will come to me," I said.

I walked inside and was heading toward the kitchen when something caught my attention in the living room. There was now over the ever-roaring fire something different. Instead of more and more books, there was what looked like a TV. I mindlessly walked by it and had to do a double take. I went back to inspect it more closely. Upon inspecting it, I could definitely tell it was a screen, but it did not have any buttons. I knew televisions had been getting thinner and thinner in my time, but this was a bit extreme; it was basically paper-thin and didn't have a single cord connecting it to anything. I got a little excited. *How do you turn this thing on? I miss my soaps!* I thought eagerly. "I didn't think TV would be allowed up here!" I said as I searched the entire screen for a way to turn it on. It was mounted in such a way that you could not see the back; there was just enough room to stick your hand behind it to try and feel for buttons or possibly wires. I couldn't find a thing. It was almost spooky. It had appeared out of nowhere, and I didn't know how to use it. Out of frustration I stomped down on the couch and stared at the screen, trying all sorts of sayings to get it to turn itself on. "Hocus-pocus! Alakazam! *On!* Start? Something? Anything!"

After I had stared at the blank, dark screen for a prolonged period of time, it out of the blue came to life. "What is this?" I said as it startled me from my stupor. What began to play was like a scene straight from a movie. I recognized it to be the accident that had occurred the day I died. I could see myself approaching the car with the two men. As I watched myself, I started to realize how bizarre the situation was and how odd they were acting. Next I saw myself walking back to the car, but one of the men was following me, and following a swift, sharp hit to the back of my head, he swept what looked like my lifeless body from the frozen asphalt into his arms. He looked in both directions and called for his friend for help with moving me. They popped open the trunk of my own car and flung me in. One man turned around and was headed back to his own car; he tore open the back door and violently grasped for the child. The boy was screaming as he was snatched from the vehicle, trying desperately to escape the clutches of the shorter man, and he was thrown into the back seat of my car. All the while they had been screaming obscenities at him, making the little boy more and more visibly upset. I could hear it clearly: "Boy, if you don't shut the hell up, we are going to kill you like we did your good-for-nothin' mama!"

Horrified, I was glued to the screen, only to watch them peel away in my car, leaving their own behind, without a care in the world. Then the screen faded to black again. My mind was reeling with the images now burned into my memory. How horrible, how evil. Who were these men? Who was that little boy? The situation was so unfamiliar, much different than I had remembered.

"Little brother, my ass!" I screamed out loud. "How dare they? How could they? What the fuck happened to me? Where did they take me?" I was so overwhelmed with anger I pounded my fists on the screen, demanding an answer. What I had just seen had rattled me to my core. I felt my body begin to shake from head to toe. As I filled with rage, I threw my head back and screamed at the top of my lungs, with tears flooding down my cheeks, until the room went black.

CHAPTER 4

The sound of the birds chirping, as they usually did in the mornings, roused me from my slumber. This time it had not been a refreshing sleep. I woke with a slightly more muted sense of anger, this time directed toward myself more than the culprits behind my evident death. I angrily kicked at the sheets that had begun to overheat me; I had to take it out on something. Then it dawned on me: "How do I keep ending up here?" I tore out of bed and stomped straight into the living room.

The monitor was still there, and it was black. "So that wasn't a nightmare," I said with the small shred of hope left inside me, wishing to unsee the past. The anguish I had to work through, the anguish that Gabe was trying to get me to recall, was now clear. "I really wish that had been just a nightmare or some cheesy horror movie," I said, and I dropped my head to my chest and stroked my own hair to soothe myself.

"Nope," Gabe said from the kitchen.

I leaped out of my skin, jolted backward, and gasped.

"Jesus Christ! Don't do that!" I could hear the thunder crackle above, but this time it wasn't so far off in the distance. In fact, it sounded as if it was directly over my home, causing the house to rumble.

"I told you not to say that; he doesn't like that sort of thing." He scolded me.

"Screw him right now! What the hell just happened; why was I shown this?" I yelled as I dramatically motioned toward the screen. "Is that all he wanted me to see? Just a big 'FYI, you were wacked mafia-style!' "

"You were shown that because you are ready to see it; it was time, and this is what will make you complete your transition. By the way, don't say 'screw him' either— that's just bad form," Gabe said in a smug and condescending tone.

"But how does that even help me? I now only have more questions than answers. Who are they? Who is the boy? Where did they take us? If they killed me, did they kill the boy too?"

"No," he said, cutting me off.

"No? No to what?" I snapped back irritated.

"No. Just no," he said.

"You are *not* helping!" I yelled at him.

"Calm down, Carol, or you will be going down for another nap." With that statement I cringed at his ability to so easily accomplish this. It took some time and a few deep breaths for me to calm down enough to begin to form coherent thoughts and sentences again. "Let us take a walk, shall we?" he said as he ushered me to the door.

"But I'm not dressed." I laughed at him.

"Yes you are."

I laughed again, then looked down, almost soiling myself with the dramatic change of attire. I was in fact dressed. But how? I had been in my pajamas and was now in day clothes, but I hadn't felt a thing. "How the hell did they sneak a bra on me without me noticing?" I looked up at Gabe and back down to my own clothes; I looked at him with suspicion. "How? Did you do this? Did you see anything? How is it even possible? Even shoes! You even got me in shoes!"

With just a sly smile, he motioned again to the door. "Come."

We stepped outside into the beautiful sunlight and onto the path, a perfectly laid yellow brick pathway that led through meadows and into the distant mountains before it disappeared from sight. "Yellow brick?" I mused "As in 'Follow the yellow brick road?' " I asked. I had yet to leave my happy little haven to venture off the porch. It didn't seem like it was necessary. I was perfectly content and comfortable where I was.

"That's what you wanted, isn't it? I don't know why else you would ask me such an odd question. If it makes you feel better, you are not the only one that has yellow brick. I personally do not understand the appeal. It's quite hideous."

With Gabe having effectively distracted me from our walk's original purpose, which had yet to be disclosed, I had to ask, "You do not see the appeal of the yellow brick road? It's iconic and comforting; it's from a movie I grew up with."

"*Movie.* I have heard that term before but do not have the slightest idea what it is; I am told it is similar in concept to what you have just seen." This statement jolted me back to why we were on our little walk.

"Yeah, it's like that, except way better because it actually makes sense. Why was I shown what happened at the accident but nothing more? And spare me the transition crap. I get it, but how does just that little bit really help me?"

With that same sly grin, he said, "I am glad you asked. You were only shown what you can handle; the accident was such a traumatic experience for you that you were only able to see just that small amount for now. This brings me to why I am here. As you have seen, your journey is not as easy as you originally thought it would be. Your soul has far to grow, and you need to know where you came from to grow to your full potential. You see, your soul knows what happened to you in your accident up until the very end, when it came here. Though your body may have been unconscious, your soul never sleeps. To better explain it, your soul is actually immortal; you have lived many past lives and will endure many more lives to come after you have completed your journey as Carol. It's as if your soul is an aspect of time—it never stops, it never sleeps, it continues on forever and is recycled through many cycles of life, death, and rebirth. At the end of your journey at this level, you will be able to unlock your full memory from all your previous lives, you will know what lies ahead of you in your next life, and you will be able to transcend and join the others before you decide to be reborn. That is the biggest decision you will ever face as you will be able to see whether your next life on Earth will be a pleasant one or not. On your journey to get to that point, you will meet and befriend many on the same path. Some take longer to find their way than others, but eventually you all make it to rebirth."

"Others? I guess that makes sense, I didn't think heaven would be so empty, but I have grown to love the silence. Where are all these other souls?" I asked.

"The others are on various parts of their own journey. Because conventional space and time do not exist here, they are all here but in their own dimension. This is the best way I can describe it to you. They can help you along the way, but they can also hurt you," he said in a dropped tone.

"Hurt me?" I asked, shocked at the idea.

"Hurt you in the sense that they will distract you from your own path or scare you from continuing on to find your way. Not hurt you in the physical sense because you do not have a physical body to harm. You see, souls are neither inherently good nor inherently evil but rather only vessels, empty ones filled by what life had to offer in that cycle. Good and evil is a concept only found on Earth to describe the actions of individuals. This is formed based off what your society finds socially acceptable, but what one society has found to be acceptable, others do not agree with, thus giving each culture its own identity and norms, but all these preconceived notions are removed once you have crossed over. These souls you will meet along the way you may already know. Some you probably encountered in your life cycle. When you have fully completed the process, you will know everyone around you—the connectivity, or should I say bond, will be akin to that of siblings."

"That sounds awesome, actually, but how long do you think it will take me to get to that phase?"

"As I have said, time does not exist here, not in the way you are still used to. Once you have completed your transition, you will no longer need the setting you are currently enjoying," he said, motioning to the beautiful countryside we were walking through. We had made our way to a more wooded pathway and were approaching an area that looked ancient and untouched for centuries (if that were even possible). The trees were covered in moss and climbing vines; most had tipped to their sides and were in various stages of decay. There was a half-covered stone monument of some sort buried deep in vegetation. Symbols covered some of the visible sides, but they were not any I recognized. I wanted badly to investigate the site more, but Gabe continued on, so I marked the site in my mind so I could go back to it.

"You will be in a place where there is neither a sunrise nor a sunset; you will no longer fear or worry or have any need for anger or hate. This is the true 'heaven' people on Earth wish to obtain but do not realize the journey it takes to reach it. Everyone eventually does transcend into this place; some need more encouragement than others, and some stay for much longer than others."

"So we reach a place of, shall we say, enlightenment, where we know everything and everyone and feel the connection between all beings, then we trade that in for a fresh start on Earth that will leave us clueless as to what we have gone though and already grown to know?" I couldn't help but think, *No wonder people stick around up here; why would they want to leave something pure for another round in the mud?*

"Yes and no. Eventually, as your soul has come to know its many past lives, there will be knowledge kept and stored within your human brain; this knowledge has yet to be tapped and developed by your scientists, mostly because they do not realize it is even there. Humans currently only use around 10 percent of their capacity, while in heaven, they use 100 percent. But there are exceptions in each life cycle; there are some who appear to be wise beyond their years, some because life events have caused them to be so, others because they retain some memories that most people either disregard, block, or can never access in their lifetimes. Humans tend to fear what they do not understand, and since past life information can be confusing or alarming, it is chalked up to a bad dream or something of the sort. The more in tune a human stays with their consciousness, the more likely they will be able to tap into their past life experiences or the knowledge they acquired here."

"So, psychics?"

"*No!* Not them, not typically. Once in a while, you will get someone who is not a fraud, but those people usually remain off the beaten path. These people are typically quiet and reserved. Traits most often associated with wisdom. They do not find the need to be boisterous or loud or claim things they do not fully understand."

"Ah, I get it." I nodded along. "What about all the people with their stories of heaven and hell? Where did they get those ideas from?"

"The same place most imaginative people get their information from—within their own minds. No one has come here and gone back to talk about it, I promise you that. Petra is good about that sort of thing."

"So when people see angels and demons and ghosts on Earth, what are they really seeing, if anything at all? Because to be honest with you, I definitely believed in ghosts when I was on Earth; too many creepy things had happened to me not to believe in something of the sort."

"There are many things people do not understand on Earth due to the limited capabilities of their own minds, as well as what we are capable of doing after death. There are many who do not accept their new sur-roundings here and are able to go back, in some ways, to Earth, in order to help them further along in their own transition. Now these souls may have found them-selves to be so bad in life or so horribly disfigured from an accident, whether imaginary or real, that they trans-form themselves into what down on Earth you would call a demon or ghost. These specters are based off preconceived images of that soul's own creativity; these demons or what have you only exist because of those souls unable to accept the truth of their new existence.

Now angels, on the other hand, are a little bit different. As I have told you, I have been assigned to you; what I did not tell you is that I have been assigned to you your whole life. You have not met me until now because he has not deemed it necessary for me to intervene. There are a select few who have seen their caretakers—or as they call them, angels—but fewer than have claimed to see them. Again, like those who transform their image into that of demons, there are those who transform themselves into angels; these are not caretakers but rather souls trying to transition. Those souls who portray themselves as angels do so to help their families or friends cope with their loss. Does that make sense?"

"Yeah," I said as I stared at him like a deer in the headlights; he had taught me so much at this point that I barely had room to store all the information.

"I know this is a lot; I am basically telling you the majority of what you have come to believe in life is a lie. This is a difficult pill to swallow, but you must do it to move forward," he gently said as he picked a small yellow wildflower from a meadow lining the path we were taking.

The path had made its way to a clearing that contained a swing set, a very simple metal swing set made for two. We headed toward it to rest our feet. I definitely needed to sit down as the information overload was making me a little dizzy.

"Now, the way to differentiate those who were caretakers and those who have turned themselves into angels or demons is their ability to communicate. Caretakers cannot communicate on Earth; they can only show up for support, as a guiding light, so to speak. Something to help grant serenity in a time of need, even if the situation doesn't seem like it would merit such intervention. It may be a preemptive visit before that life is dramatically altered."

"So have you ever been sent down to Earth to do that? Is that just something you do when you see fit or when called upon to do it?"

With a long pause and a deep sigh, Gabe slowly responded with "Ah, yes. Just once, as I said; very few times has this needed to occur."

"Why did you need to go?"

"I was summoned down to help someone."

"Yes, I get that, but what could have possibly happened that required intervention?"

"Oh, the details are irrelevant; I was summoned to show the correct path she was to take. Things had not gone as planned."

"That is what I am not understanding. If things are predestined, how can things not go as planned?"

"Humans are able to alter their lives as they please; every outcome is interconnected. We know what will happen. This particular occasion warranted some help."

"But if you know how it is supposed to happen, why—"

"Moving on," Gabe stated very abruptly, making it clear he did not want to talk about that subject any longer. So naturally I made a mental note to bring that one back up. "I was telling you the souls that decide to become and transform themselves into what they think are angels or demons have had difficulty accepting their surroundings. They then go back to Earth and attempt to make contact with someone close to them in life. However, what they do not realize is that time here is not as it was on Earth and they are decades if not centuries late in some cases. I believe that is why people have 'haunted houses,' or whatever they are fashionably known as on Earth."

"Centuries! It takes some souls *that* long to get it through their skulls?"

With a disgruntled sigh, he said, "Yes, unfortunately it takes some people that long. They do eventually find their way; some require extensive coaching to get back to a more human form. Be warned, you will meet them along your journey; they may seem scary, but that is how they feel they should look. Do you understand your surroundings a little bit better?"

Looking around, I said, "Yeah, I used to have this exact swing set as a kid. I didn't realize how much I missed it."

"Not that! I mean what I have told you about your soul and all the souls around you!"

"Oh! Yeah! *That.* Gotcha. We are good. No need to shout, really. Or get snippy." The last part I said under my breath.

"I heard that; but we will push forward," he said as he tossed his hair to the one side. I could tell he definitely did that intentionally, a little "look at me, look at me," in my opinion. I tried to mimic him and almost fell off the swing. "I came here to help you through your death. Tell me in your own words what you can remember and where you would like to start."

Fidgeting as if I were a schoolchild summoned to the principal's office, I said, "Well, I guess I should start with the fact that I had not realized what had happened on the day of the accident. Before the replay was shown to me, I basically assumed I had died in an accident on my way to work. I didn't think much about it because I knew I could not change what had already been done. But now I see it was not at all like that. In fact, I don't have a clue if I was dead when they dragged me back into my own car or if I died somewhere else and never knew about it. So to answer your question, I would like to start with knowing why they killed me and where I actually died."

Gabe nodded his head in silence for a while, to the point of awkwardness, then finally broke his silence to say, "That is a great place to start, and you will need to be brave; are you up for knowing the details?"

This time it was my turn to ponder and pause. I finally made up my mind to say softly, "Yes, I would like to know."

"Great!" He said as he jumped off the swing and yanked me with him. "We begin as soon as you are ready!"

Within a blink of an eye, we were back in my home; his head was in my fridge, yet again, and he grabbed an apple. I was so disoriented from the change of scenery I thought I was going to get violently ill. It was as if when he yanked me off the swing he had pulled me through a wormhole back into my own home; I was hunched over the edge of the couch trying to get my vision back in line. With his mouth full, he sloppily said, "You are going to want to get some sleep; when I see you next, you are going to be overwhelmed. Mm, this one is juicy! What do you call this fruit again?"

I looked at him from over the side of the couch with what I can only assume was a very pale yet very green look on my face as the little yank he had given me had definitely twisted my insides into knots. The only response to his question I could muster were odd gurgling noises and possibly a whimper.

"Ah, maybe next time. Off to bed you go; you will feel better soon, and we will have work to do," he said as he grabbed me by my shoulders and led me to my own bed. I looked down to see I had been changed into my pajamas, a parlor trick I was not yet fond of. Before I could even protest, I was tucked in, he had disappeared, and my eyes became impossible to keep open. I gave up trying to fight it. Within seconds I was out cold, again.

CHAPTER 5

"Ugh, I hate it when he does that!" I groaned as I rolled over to get out of bed. I quickly dressed myself with a sense that if I didn't do it, I would look down and someone else would have done it to me. (That thought still didn't sit well with me; it creeped me out, to be honest.) When I was satisfied with the attire I had chosen, I went for my morning coffee. "I wonder if he is already waiting for me in my kitchen?" As I walked into the room, trying not to make any noise so I could sneak up on him, and peered around the corner into the kitchen, I saw my typical spread laid out in front of me—the piping hot coffee on the counter, and not a speck of dirt in sight, but no Gabe. *Hmm*, I thought. I figured he would be eating all my apples by now, apples I had still never seen in the fridge. "Oh, well," I said as I grabbed my coffee and continued my morning routine of watching the sun come up outside, all the while thinking that if he really was all-knowing, he would know I was out there and waiting for him.

I finished my coffee, anxiously waiting for him to show up. I went back inside and proceeded to grab a book; I had to get my mind off him. The best thing I could do was my usual routine—until he decided to grace me with his presence. I curled up on the couch with a book.

What I could only assume was hours later, with me halfway through my book, my stomach gurgled. Feeding time! I wanted some chicken parmesan, so off to the oven I went to grab my meal, and when I sat down to eat and go over the story I had just been reading in my head, I realized my mind was completely blank. I could only think of the story that was my life, my last memories—that is, my death. All that time I had spent reading I had not absorbed a single word. My anxiety was so high I could only truly think, *When will he get here? What will I find out today? Who is behind this?* After eating, I plopped back down on the couch and grabbed the book again. I stared at the cover and then threw it aside. "What's the point? I am way too anxious to try now. Where is that guy! Shouldn't he be here by now?" All questions and no answers to any of them—it was killing me. I hated not knowing. So I stood up and started to pace. "Maybe this will get him here faster, making it obvious I need him."

I paced until the sun went down and finally allowed myself to take a seat. I waited and waited until I could not stand it anymore. Though I could not bring myself to leave the couch or do anything, in case he showed up. "I need to know what is happening! He said he would come when I was ready, so where is he? I am definitely ready." There was not a peep in return. I finally gave up and went to bed. "Maybe tomorrow," I muttered as I began to fling my clothes off and into the general vicinity of the closet, this time not caring who saw me naked—after all, it was my house, damn it.

Days went by with the same anxious waiting. The longer I waited, the less interested in wanting to know what happened and the more interested in wishing I were back to my old routine I became. It finally got to the point where I gave up waiting altogether and went completely back to the schedule I loved. Now I added a little adventure to my days by going for a walk. I was dying (no pun intended) to check out those fascinating ruins Gabe and I had encountered on our walk. It did not take long for me to find them, though it was odd—they did not appear when I wanted them to, in the manner of everything else in my heaven. These I had to search for. So, after a little hike, I found my reward. Just as it had appeared the other day—the large stone structure reminded me of Stonehenge but was far more detailed in design. My curiosity led me to investigate; I think it was a subconscious excuse for me to take my mind off my impending visitation from Gabe, who would come when he pleased, apparently. I laughed to myself.

I walked around the whole structure, tripping over fallen stones that were hidden under dense vines and shrubs. I ran my fingers over the designs etched into the stones—or were they etched words? I could not tell. I felt like a little archaeologist on my very first dig. I started to pull away the shrubs and the vines to reveal more design and better-preserved stones. I would stare in fascination and marvel at the beauty of it until it started to get dark, then I would head home. I couldn't believe how smooth some of the stones still were, as if they had never been touched by the elements. Some showed signs of paint, slight blue and red hues; I found it so fascinating that I had never seen symbols quite like them. I played Indiana Jones for a few days, and the thought of Gabe popped in and out of my head. Something I still could not understand is why he would say we would begin and then disappear on me again. Like a bad boyfriend. I didn't appreciate being stood up like that.

I continued to go back to the ruins I was fascinated by, but I went back better equipped each time. Some days I would go with a shovel or some excavation tools I had managed to find in the little shed around the back of my house. Cute little shed built to look like a small barn. It only had one or two things in it and probably hadn't even been there the whole time. I felt like it had popped itself into existence when I started my little adventure! On other days I would take books from the shelves that looked the most pertinent to what I was trying to find. I couldn't find much about the ruins in any of the books, but I scoured them every night, trying to match the images I was seeing with ones documented. Yet I could not find a single thing resembling the stones; there was always a significant difference between the ruins and the book illustrations.

I spent days, possibly even weeks, trying to find

information about the ruins, only to arrive at more questions than answers. The result was me staring at the site and coming up with wild stories in my head about how the stones gotten there. After long days of digging and staring, I would walk back home. Though the walk back always appeared to be shorter, this was definitely not the case. Something about the ruins intrigued me; they seemed to defy all the typical luxuries I had grown accustomed to in heaven. I could not put my finger on it, but I was bound and determined to figure it out. One of the wild stories I had dreamed up was that there were natives in what I had grown to call heaven. They had been there long before it was taken over for the purpose it held now. The ruins I was looking at only belonged here and not on Earth; they would never have existed on Earth because their maker was never there. I loved this idea so much I adopted it as truth, but to be certain, I needed to make sure nothing like this existed on Earth, so I continued my quest to prove myself right.

One morning, with coffee in hand as I began my routine, I went to my bookshelves. I scanned the shelves for anything I might have missed before. Deep in concentration, I flipped through the books, and then I heard from the kitchen, "You already know you are not going to find the answers in there." Gabe was speaking.

Throwing my mug in the air as I grabbed my chest and let out a muffled scream, I said, "Damn it, Gabe! Why do you do that to me? Where the hell have you even been!"

"Very good, Carol; you are slowly learning not to

offend him. Besides, you know I am only here to help. It is not like I am going to kill you or anything," he said with a sly smirk on his face.

"Whatever," I said, irritated as I looked at the massive mess the splattered coffee and shattered mug had made. "Please tell me this is going to clean itself up."

"You already know it will," he said with his mouth full of apple.

"How do you keep finding those in the fridge? I never eat them, and they aren't in there when I look. It is always empty if I do not wish anything to be in there."

"You would be surprised. Are you happy with my cleaning job?" he said as I looked around and saw the space was as spotless as it had been before. Even on my sweater, there was not a single drop.

"Yes, you are the greatest maid, even with the stealing food from the fridge and everything. Perfectly done. So are you here to help me with figuring out those ruins we saw on our walk?"

"Huh? No. I am here to help you on your way to figure out how you got here. Besides, silly girl, those you are not going to figure out in any of the little books you have on your shelves. You will need to visit the library for that!" he said with a small chuckle.

"Library? There is a library?" It seemed too pedestrian to have something like a library up here.

"Yes, ma'am, and we are headed there today."

I was thrilled yet nervous. *I get to see more!* There were so many questions I had for Gabe, yet the idea of a library didn't seem like it was going to cut it. Why would the information I needed to find out be in a library? I needed questions answered by people who were still living, people who knew why it happened and how it happened and who else was involved. I didn't even know when I died. Was it when I was so carelessly tossed in my own trunk, or was it later down the road? Maybe it was even literally down the road! *How will a library be able to answer that for me?* It was shocking how quickly my mind jumped back into gear on the subject. I was so focused on my new fascination I had blocked out the main focus of speaking with Gabe up to that point.

"Calm down; this is not a library like you are used too," Gabe said as he nonchalantly read my mind. "This is the library all libraries are based on—having some idea of what you are looking for or even just where to begin will help you. You see, libraries are places that contain vast amounts of knowledge; they are there for anyone to go to and learn within. Since time does not exist here, as I have mentioned, this library is constantly evolving and so large you will not feel it is crowded."

"Crowded?" I said with a twinge of anxiety.

"Well, yes, there is only one library in all of heaven. Only one is needed, and it houses all knowledge held on heaven and on Earth. It contains all memories recorded from the start of time and knows what will come; the trick is to find it. That is a much more difficult task. The library is a journey on its own. Getting there is the easy part; trying to find answers will take a long time. Remember why you are there. There is so much knowledge and information. Anything you could ever possibly want to know will be there for you to find."

"Ok. So how do we get there, great Yoda?"

"Yoda? What is a 'Yoda'?"

Smirking, I said, "Never mind. I am ready to go to the library; lead the way. Will I need a pass or something?"

"No. No pass, not like on Earth," he said in a serious tone. I didn't have the heart to tell him I was joking. One thing I definitely noticed—he did *not* understand sarcasm, or at least my particular brew. He took everything so literally yet was so sassy. I wonder if sarcasm was an Earth thing; maybe a sense of humor was also an Earth thing. It was too hard to tell, but I definitely didn't want to let mine go.

We headed out the door as if we were going for a walk again, yet this time a new path was there for us to follow. This path led away from the ruins and was definitely not there before. It was still paved with yellow bricks, which made me smile. It led over a small hill that I could not see beyond. This expedition was thrilling and had my heart pounding—whether it was pounding from excitement or fear, I did not know, but I wasn't going to let it stop me. Hell, with how sporadically I saw Gabe, if I didn't go now, who knew when I would see him next to guide me! Next century, maybe?

I tried to block that last thought, so he didn't think I felt resentment, even though I kind of did. So I tried to change the subject. "That's odd."

"As you have already seen, when you are ready, things will appear to you. So this new path is one you are ready to follow," he said as we started on our way, not mentioning a word about what I can only assume he had read from my mind. The path leading to the small hill was calm and serene, nothing but brush and wildflowers amid a nice, cool breeze, but when we got to the top of the hill, the scene took my breath away.

Sprawled out beneath us was what appeared to be a small town centralized around an exceedingly large building that dwarfed any other building tenfold. It was a breathtaking sight to behold; it was something like a city made of light. We were starting down toward the central building when my yellow brick path turned into cobblestone. Though the street was paved with stone, you could almost walk on it barefoot; it was so clean it could have been made of tile or wood and be set in a home interior. There were some on the streets selling goods and shopping, as if this were a flourishing metropolis, although upon closer inspection it did not seem as if there was any money exchanging hands, and not even bartering. As we walked through the streets and approached some of these stands, which were selling all sorts of items, including produce and grains, clothes and beautiful jewels, I could not help but notice that the items requested were just given away, only paid for with a thank you and a smile. "How strange," I said aloud to myself.

"How so?"

"Well, no one is paying for anything; how do these merchants stay in business?"

"These souls are here because they want to be. They

do not need anything in return for their services as they are doing this purely for their own enjoyment. You found solace in your books and your walks to the site of the ruins; they find it in talking with others like themselves and selling the fruit of the trades they had grown to love in life."

"I see. I did not expect to see people working here. I figured that was just an earthly necessity."

"Well, it is. The people selling do not need to do so; they want to. And those purchasing the goods do not need to do so; they find enjoyment in walking around the marketplace shopping. As I mentioned in regard to your books, heaven is quite different for each soul; these were more social in life and do not wish to give that up. It brought them the most joy."

It all did make sense and was nice to see. I hadn't realized how much I had missed people. I have always preferred solitude with a pet to being with others in a social setting, but it was still nice to see others.

We pressed on and made our way onto large open lawns with trees of every type; some animals were there, lounging on the grass—animals of all sorts, actually. The sun shone down on the place to illuminate every nook and cranny; there was not a single spot of shade unless you were underneath a tree. There were fountains and statues everywhere; everything was so well maintained. Every person, or should I say, soul, you could see was healthy and happy; not a single individual looked in need of anything, not a sad face in the lot. The most magnificent thing of all was what I could only assume was the library, exceedingly large and so ancient yet as timeless as everything surrounding it. The library was not just a library, though; it was attached to a light-house. This part, though beautiful, struck me as odd yet extremely familiar, but I couldn't put my finger on why.

"This lighthouse, my dear, is meant to be a beacon to guide all the needy souls to the library of knowledge. You like history; do you recognize this place?"

It took me a bit of time to even understand what he was asking. How could I recognize this based off my interest in history? Was this place on Earth? If it was on Earth, how did it get here? Didn't he already say no one has made it to heaven and back to tell the tale, let alone get so far as to snag a glimpse of this magnificent beast and get back to make a duplicate? So I searched my mind and scanned the building again. Large ancient building made of what looked like marble or some similar, light-colored stone, and a lighthouse. "Nope, not ringing a bell."

"Look more closely; maybe something will stand out," he said.

I gave it another shot. As we came closer to the library, I began to notice little things standing out, like the statues and fountains, which seemed to be based on Greek mythology. Yet the design clearly showed signs of Egyptian architecture; the sheer size alone reminded me of the grandeur sought out by the Egyptian pharaohs. The lighthouse seemed to be in three sections—the first, a square; the second, an octagon; and the last section circular with a beacon of fire raging at the top. This little game started to intrigue me. As we approached the entrance, large and grand as it was, I looked up at the figure adorning the lighthouse. *Could that be what I think it is?* I thought to myself. "Could that really be?"

"Ahh, you finally got it; that statue up top there is what gave it away, didn't it?" Gabe confirmed with a grin.

"Is that?" I paused. "Is that what I think it is?"

"Yes, that is a statue of Poseidon (or Zeus; I can never remember which is which); but yes, that would be the Lighthouse of Alexandria. Seemed too fitting of a beacon to let such a wonderful piece of Earth history go to waste."

"Oh, my. So wait, does that mean the library is *the* library? The one that was burned down with all its scrolls and history?"

"Yes, the Lighthouse and Library of Alexandria in all their glory are now here; they were repurposed when their ability to unite and educate people was replaced with greed, among other things," he said, seemingly depressed and yet disappointed. "As you can see, the lighthouse is fully operational and the library is large enough to accommodate you if you feel the need to stay here until you are able to get the answers you seek. I must again advise you to keep in mind why you are here and always retain that goal. Yes, this place is magnificent, and even I can get lost among the books, scrolls, and wealth of knowledge you will encounter, but you will quickly find this place can also become a trap you can easily get sucked into."

We made our way into the library, passing through

its glorious threshold lined with marble statues of the mythological greats—some were a little more obscure than others. The whole interior was filled with shelf upon shelf of the written word, everywhere, separated only by columns and sitting areas, leaving not a barren wall in sight. The place was silent; you could hear a pin drop. So we proceeded with caution, so as not to disturb the others on their own journeys and adventures. Gabe hadn't been kidding when he had said the place could be full of people but was so large that I wouldn't have felt it. I could sense others around us, but it was as if they were wisps in the air, barely seen, as if only for a moment.

There were rows of desks lining a main aisle, and to the left were rooms, seemingly conference rooms, with large desks; some were bigger than others, but all were filled with souls. I couldn't help but stare. It was the most interaction I had seen in quite a while, and I have always been a people watcher by nature, so naturally I gawked. On the right were laboratories of all sorts. Some looked like chemistry labs, with all their beakers and burners; others looked like clean rooms with large machinery and souls in hazmat suits. This made me chuckle, because seriously, what were they afraid of? They were already dead! Lastly, some simply were laid out like classrooms.

My eyes wandered upward; from inside I could recognize that the whole base of the lighthouse was the library, with a spiral staircase starting from the back of the main floor and leading all the way to the top, lining the inside of exterior walls, completely enveloping you within its walls of the written word. These wraparound stairs narrowed as the lighthouse tapered off from a square into an octagonal structure. What made it so amazing was that books lined the entire span of the stairway to the top floor. There was no need for a ladder, because you could simply climb the stairs to get to the book you needed. This was even more awe inspiring when you incorporated the intermittent frescos and statues. Depictions of every deity from all of time, most of whom I did not recognize, but it didn't take more than a moment to catch onto the theme. Some items were quite crude, rough carvings of stone or clay, while others were so lifelike you felt as if you could see them breathe or even see the hair moving in the breeze. We came across one which caught my eye: this one I knew from life. A brief visit as a child to a Smithsonian museum flashed back to me while I gravitated to and stood dwarfed by its magnificent size and majestic detail. As a kid I remembered this painting to be worn away from the cruel nature of time, but here, I could actually smell the slight rancidity of oil-based paint.

The stairs had a couple of landings before you hit the top. Each landing led to a hall and had rooms, but these rooms you could not see into. They appeared to contain closed-door, private sessions. It was hard to tell without breaking free from my tour to venture up and find out. The higher one climbed, the older and more intriguing the lighthouse became. "Can we go up there?" I begged Gabe like a schoolgirl.

"That is exactly where we are headed—up the stairs, second door on your left."

I was filled with mixed emotions. I was excited to go in deeper, but the thought of what was waiting for me behind those doors filled me with fear, excitement, and anxiety. What, exactly, was I about to find, or whom? As we made our way closer to the stairs, I could see in greater detail the engravings on the columns, and they appeared to be hieroglyphics; what I could see was definitely ancient Egyptian in origin. The symbols were scrawled on everything from the columns to the hand-rail of the stairs. As I ran my hand over the intricate symbols, I wondered what they meant.

"It says, 'Through knowledge we gain the strength of one thousand armies and the wisdom of all mankind, and only then can we conquer death, our only adversary.' He thought it was too fitting to remove."

"I see," I said as I noticed that as we climbed, the writing all around us, even on the columns, began to change. The design was not nearly as intricate, which led me to believe the higher we went, the older the script became. It started to look like a sequence of gashes in the railing, like geometric shapes. *How could anyone ever read that?* I thought.

"You are looking at Sumerian; not many even understand what that means, but you do. Look at the detail work. It may seem crude, but it is in fact very intricate."

I was stunned at the detail and complexity of the Sumerian language. I had only seen it in books, and in that format, I had never been able to fathom how small and precise it all really was. I ran my hands over the cuneiform text a little more delicately than I had the hieroglyphs, as if I could somehow wipe away the past or damage the text. I needed to know more about this. I made a mental note to go back through my books at home to research and hopefully learn what it all said. Being so fixated on the detailed handrail, I hardly paid attention to what was directly in front of me. I nearly slammed into Gabe as he stopped at the top of the stairs, or should I say, second-level landing.

"Crap!" I said with a start and stumbled. Clutching the handrail as I shifted backward, dangerously close to tumbling down the stairs, I leveled myself in panic and let go of the railing as quickly as possible. Feeling guilty for possibly damaging the railing, I glared at Gabe and inspected the rail for possible damage. "You could have signaled, you know! Put on a brake light or something."

He did not seem amused, with a look on his face that signaled he meant business—more so than usual. "This is where I leave you to your adventure. As I said, second door on the left; that is where you will begin. Always remember why you are here. If you look below you, those are the souls who have trapped themselves here, unable to move forward because they are too fascinated with what is directly in front of them. They do not realize, whether intentionally or not, that all the knowledge they seek will come to them once they have transitioned above." With that said, and with a wave of his hand, he ushered me toward my destination.

With a deep gulp and sweaty palms, I stepped past

him and headed toward the closed door; now even more than before I was filled with anxiety and fear. I could not help but think about what had been so hard that all those people below me had not been able to face it and had decided to dwell below? After a few steps, I turned to thank him, only to find he was gone. Shouldn't have been a surprise at this point, but it was unsettling nonetheless.

I stood directly in front of the door for quite a while. I studied every inch of its exquisite detail, from the hand-carved wood accents to the bronze door handle, simple in design, no doubt as ancient as the rest of the lighthouse, yet so well maintained, as if it had never been used. I couldn't hear a single thing, not even a peep from another room, absolute silence. I even stuck my ear to the door to see if I could hear someone waiting for me on the other side, but I could not hear anything or anyone. I could see through the cracks that a light was on the other side, a soft, yellow glow, warm and inviting, yet I could not shake the feeling that everything was going to change for me. So I stood there. I stood there until I could muster the courage to continue forward.

"That's it. I'm doing this!" I said loudly, trying to psych myself up enough to go for it. I grabbed the handle as firmly as I could, and with a scream in my head and my full weight against the door, I shoved my way in.

CHAPTER 6

I opened my eyes after taking a deep breath, terrified at what I would find; my heart was racing as I quickly scanned the room. The room was lit with one lamp; it illuminated the space well enough without being over-powering. All that was in the room was one lounge chair in the center of a round area rug and a small wooden end table holding the lamp omitting the soft yellow glow. The room itself was quite large in size, too large for the meager furniture within. The furniture seemed out of character with the building. I would have expected more opulence in a place like this, but it was more to the taste and style I had grown used to in life; it had more of a nostalgic Americana feel to it, even the lamp.

The chair was set facing the wall on the left, so naturally I went toward the chair, circled around to see if I had missed anything hiding in any of the shaded corners, and then sat down when I felt at ease. I looked up to see another monitor; I had totally missed this one because it was completely flush against the wall.

Like someone had stuck a piece of black paper to the wall. *I can't believe I missed that,* I thought. The chair was comfortable enough, for such an uncomfortable situation. It felt like I was waiting to get into the principal's office, my stomach twisting and turning into knots. *This room will change my life?* I could not believe that such an unassuming setting could change how I lived in my day-to-day life—well, "life." My own thoughts made me chuckle; I had to do something to ease my anxiety. I had no idea what was coming my way, and honestly it completely freaked me out.

As I sat there, my eyes wandered around the room, and when I got bored, my mind began to wander— mostly to what I was going to eat for dinner, how a great big club sandwich would do the trick. Then it wandered off to the ruins near the house and whether the books below would be able to help me hunt down their origin. It had begun to feel like hours had passed when out of nowhere the screen in front of me began to show an image. This jolted me back to reality. "Holy crap. How long have I been daydreaming?" I said with a start.

It began like an old news reel, hazy and grainy at first, and then began to clear up. The screen was showing a house, one that had seen better days, shabby and unkept. It was white with black shudders, or should I say, at one point it had been white with black shudders. Half the shudders were off at least one of their hinges; the white paint on the house was dingy and peeling. There were vines crawling wildly along the whole front of the house, and even the gutters looked like little planters with sprouts coming out of them. The front yard was an overgrown catastrophe, but from the looks of the surrounding houses, this one was the pick of the litter. The house to the left was burned out, while the house to the right had plastic over the windows, which bellowed in the breeze. In the cracked driveway, there was a bright red sedan, very out of character with the rest of the neighborhood. As I looked more closely, I realize it was my car! "What the hell!" I leaped forward in my chair. I needed to inspect the car to make sure it was definitely mine. I could see the bumper sticker: "White's Dealership, Home of the Greats." Oh, it definitely was mine. I felt my face light up with rage, turning bright red like a Christmas decoration. I was livid about their blatant carelessness toward my car!

One of the men emerged from the house; he looked thinner and shabbier than I remembered. Maybe it was because he was without a coat, or maybe because this time the house didn't do his looks any favors. He looked around, making sure no eyes were watching him, and then unlocked the trunk—or should I say, *my* trunk. Before he opened it up all the way, he looked one last time over his shoulder, and right before my eyes, I could see my own body. The hair all over me began to stand on end. I could hardly breathe. I thought I was having a panic attack. My eyes welled with tears, and I grabbed the arm of the chair with a white-knuckled grip. I could hardly see through my own tears as the monster carelessly took my body from the trunk and half carried, half dragged me to the backyard. Clearly he was not strong enough to pick me up. He treated me like I was a sack of potatoes and not the fellow human being I was.

From around the side of the house, I watched as he lost his grip and resorted to dragging me the rest of the way to his shed. He dropped my body in front of the shed, tore open the door, and rolled me in. He tossed me around as if I were a rag doll; he then frantically reached into his pocket and pulled out a lock, which he put on the latch. Having checked to see if it was secure by tugging on it a few times, he began to walk away with satisfaction.

He had no regard for human life—none for my life, at least. At this point I could not hold back the tears, and they poured down my cheeks. I could tell by how lifeless my body was in his arms that I had already died. He had taken my life on the side of the road. Though my body could no longer feel the pain, my soul felt the agony now. I felt the pain deep within. I even touched my head at the point where he had struck the one and only blow necessary to snuff out my life; it was warm to the touch, as if it had just happened.

Trembling, I continued to watch the screen as he walked back to the car; he slammed the trunk shut, then went into the back seat. He stooped down and seemed to struggle with whatever he was taking from the back seat. I could hear muffled cries, and then I saw him—the little boy. I could not believe he was still alive. I wiped away my tears so as to get a better look at his precious face; seeing him alive gave me much-needed hope. The man dragged the boy out by his hair and forcibly twisted him to keep him from squirming, covering his mouth to keep him quiet. He slammed the door shut with his leg and hauled the boy into the house. The screen went black.

I could not believe what I had seen. What did they want with the boy? Who was he? Was he still alive? My journey finally became clear. It was not about me, as I had originally thought. My transition would not be complete until I understood my connection with that little boy, the little boy I knew nothing about even after the most recent revelation.

I stood up and wiped away what was left of my tears, determined to know what had happened. I staggered toward the door, not realizing how strongly the event had affected me; it had taken the strength right out of my legs, and I could hardly walk. As I reached for the handle, the screen turned back on. This time all I could see was a casket. I raced back to the screen with new-found strength and stood within inches of it so I would not miss a single second of the precious information I was being shown. The casket was covered in white flowers and was made of a dark wood, espresso in color. I could not see anything other than the casket with the flowers on top, but I could hear the crying. The crying grew louder and stronger, with muffled sniffles, and then I could hear a man speaking very clearly.

"Good evening. All, please be seated." There was a long pause, and then I could slowly make out the crying, grief-stricken crowd as the camera turned toward it. All dressed in black, with heads buried in their palms or in Kleenex. I couldn't make out the faces as they all shuffled around to sit down. "We are gathered here to commemorate Carol Armstrong's life…" My mind shut down. I went into full panic mode, and my knees began to wobble and could not hold me up any longer. His voice, before clear as day, became muffled and distant. I collapsed on the ground. I hit the edge of the chair before I tumbled and turned onto the floor. Then, darkness.

I woke up on the floor of the room—not quite what I was expecting, given that every time Gabe clocked me out, I wound up in my bed. Though I was not stiff from the fall, my head throbbed from having hit it on the chair. I touched the spot just behind my left eye where it hurt the worst and felt a lump—no blood, luckily, but, then again, would there be? I groggily rolled over to check my surroundings. To my amazement nothing had changed, no one had come for me, and nothing was out of place. Not sure why that amazed me so much; I guess I was expecting, or hoping, Gabe would come to help me, but no one was there. With the help of the chair, I pulled myself to my feet. Once I confirmed I was not hurt, I plopped back into the chair.

"Ok, time to process what I just saw. First they show me the jackass that killed me, then they torment me with hope for the little boy, and now I see my own funeral. But I don't actually see the funeral because I'm a big

chicken and freaked out over being dead—go figure."
I scolded myself as I rubbed the knot throbbing behind
my eye.

With all this new information to process, I didn't
know where to begin. "Where did he bury me? Did he
even bury me? What if my corpse is rotting in that shed
still! If that is the case, who or what was in that casket?
How did anyone find me? I never thought in a million
years my life would end this way. I had more of an adventure in the trunk of my own car, dead, than I had during
my entire life! That even includes my trip to the Grand
Canyon. This is sad."

As I sat and dwelled on my own self-pity, a little light
bulb clicked on in my head and I realized, "Wait a minute, is this even about me? Wasn't that what I was about
to do before? I need to find out what happened to that
kid! Who was he, and what did they want with him?" I
settled my thoughts and got myself together. I knew my
next steps; I needed to find out about that little boy. I
needed to save him, if I could, but where would I even
begin? They had everything down there, but how would
I even look? "It's not like they have the internet up
here," I said aloud.

"Yes we do; who do you think brought it to Earth?"
Gabe said matter-of-factly from directly behind the
chair. As usual at this point, I leaped out of my skin.

"*Stop* doing that! Or else I will ring a bell around
your neck like a cat!" I said, though I could barely hear
myself talk through the sound of my heart pounding
out of my chest. He had come into the room so silently

I hadn't even known he was there. "How long have you been standing there, anyway?" I said, trying to calm my nerves with a slow pace around the room.

"Long enough," he said before abruptly changing the subject. "So you didn't like what you saw, did you?"

"Well, of course not! I'm dead in a *shed*! Seriously? Who does that! And another thing, what did they do with that little boy? And why did I only see a glimpse of my funeral?"

"Because you passed out."

Visibly irritated, I said, "Well, ok. Then why isn't it on now so I can see the rest? Don't I still need to know what happened?"

"Because you are obviously not ready."

"Well, I am ready for it now, so show me what I need to do or how I can start the video back up. I need to know what happened. Why even show me my own funeral? What good would that do me?"

"You will see when you are ready," he said in his usual cool, collected tone.

"I am ready now! Show me!"

"Are you sure you can handle it?"

Turning red in the face, I said, "Yes, I am positive. Now show me my own life; don't you think I am entitled to know?" I couldn't contain the attitude any longer.

"If you feel you are ready." He motioned toward the screen with a sigh. That's when the screen turned on again. My pulse quickened. I couldn't hold myself up then, let alone after what I was about to see. I pawed the chair until I could lower myself into it. All the while

Gabe was staring me down. I was trying to play it cool, so I said, "Don't worry; I got this."

He scoffed and said, "Who are you trying to kid? I can read your mind, remember? Just sit down and relax. He will know when to stop."

Annoyed at the obvious, I tried to relax as the images on the screen came to life, starting at the point where I had left off. The crowd at the funeral was visible; this time I could make out the front row. Between sobs I could see the faces of my mother and sister. They both looked much older than I had remembered them. Especially my mom. She looked as if she had aged ten years since I had last seen her. *That can't be right*, I thought.

This was all so surreal. I tried to listen as the pastor continued with my eulogy. I needed to hear more, more about my own death—like what happened, who found me, where they found me, or any clue about the little boy. The pastor skirted around the issue; he only said something about me being found and that it was "an unfortunate circumstance." It made my stomach turn over. I yelled at the screen, "I was *murdered*! *Just say it!*" I couldn't bear it anymore. I was about to turn away when I noticed a face in the crowd I was not expecting to see.

It was him. He was sitting toward the back of the room, doing remarkably well at blending into the crowd. I almost did not recognize him when I saw him, especially since he was dressed up. It was clearly him, though. I couldn't believe my eyes. My own killer had snuck in and was attending my funeral! What a perverse freak! The video seemed to zoom in on his face, or maybe it seemed this way because I almost face-planted into the screen to get a better look for myself. I needed to be sure. It definitely was him—his dark brown hair, lightly bronzed skin, and cold, dark eyes. I wanted to see if I could read his facial expression. Did he feel anything seeing the pain he had caused my family and friends? Did he know how much he has made them suffer, and did he even care?

I stared unblinking at him to make sure I wouldn't miss a moment, not one single anxious look—or smile, if he was such a freak that he got his jollies from this sort of thing. His expression was blank, neither remorseful nor happy. It was unreal. He sat there stoic, completely unmoved by the sadness surrounding him. "He caused this! Why would he go there? Why would he sit through this and be unmoved? What was the purpose of that?" I wanted to scream through the screen so they could all hear me. It didn't faze me that what I was watching was already over and done with, that I couldn't change the past.

As I was too busy glaring at my killer, I missed the remaining ceremony, and they had now begun the procession to view the body. The strange thing was they had left my casket closed. He waited patiently for the others to make their way through the line. Some people left flowers on the casket; others touched it, as if the physical touch would bring them a sense of being closer. I could see the warmth from their fingers as they touched the cold, hard surface, as this left a small print or, better yet, an impression. It was as if they were giving me their warm thoughts and memories through each touch. It was finally his turn, and though others opted out of the procession, he stayed true. When he made his way to the front, he gently touched the lid and leaned forward and gave a subtle knock. Satisfied, he walked away.

Though I had only been able to see a small portion of the funeral, I had seen enough. I knew I was missed, and more importantly I had seen my killer yet again, and in the most inappropriate of places.

The screen continued to show me images; as people were waiting for the burial, I could hear them whisper to one another.

"Did you hear how she died?" asked one cousin.

"I can't believe it—ya know, about her body," mumbled a few work friends to each other.

"Did they ever find them?" a second cousin asked her mother but failed to notice *my* poor mother was within earshot.

Mom's grief-stricken response was "*No,* and they say they never will!" Under the care of my uncle, her brother, she was carried away. My killer, who had stuck around, heard this, and he didn't respond as I had thought he would. He instead responded with the subtlest facial expression; the knot he was holding between his eyebrows released its tension, and his face relaxed. This took me completely by surprise. I judged him to be a horrible monster, someone getting off on the crime, someone who was proud of himself for having done such a horrible thing, but that was not the impression he had just given. It was almost as if the weight of the world was off his shoulders. Maybe this was a reflection of not having to face justice in his lifetime. Or was it more? Was he actually remorseful for his crime?

"That could mean two things. One, he is relieved to be able to continue on without the fear of being caught. Or two, he is actually remorseful about what he has done," I said out loud, though I knew full well Gabe knew the answer and had already read my thoughts.

"Only time will tell," said Gabe.

"How?" I retorted. "Didn't you just tell me time is not the same here as it is on Earth? How exactly will I find out in time?"

"No need to be snippy, Carol. I just mean that in due time you will find the answers you seek. There is not instant gratification on this journey; you do not simply find everything in one sitting and become healed. In due time it will piece together like a puzzle, and you will be grateful to have not been bombarded with the information all at once."

This only helped a little—not quite what I was looking for, but I didn't exactly have a choice in the matter.

The screen continued to display the burial; at this point they had made it to the cemetery and were standing around the grave. My mother and sister had bought me a beautiful headstone; it had two cherubs holding a heart above the words:

Here Lies a Beloved Daughter and Sister
May God Rest Her Soul
June 23, 1973–February 17, 2019

"February seventeenth?" I was trying to remember what day that was. "You wouldn't by chance have a calendar, would you?" I asked Gabe.

He smiled at me and said, "Of course not, but that day was a Thursday."

"Thursday? That means I was in the shed slowly dying for four days!"

Before I could become too overwhelmed with grief, I heard from my gossipy cousin Ginny, whispering, "No, Stuart." She was talking to her husband. "That's just the day they assumed; well, you know what I mean."

This time my heart couldn't take it anymore. I truly had reached my limit; my poor family had been left in ruins, and they didn't even know when I had died! This was devastating. I couldn't wrap my head around it. I put my hands in my palms and just sobbed.

"Carol, there is one last thing you need to see."

I looked up and just let the tears stream down my cheeks, creating puddles on my shirt. Through huffs and blurred vision, I could see the line to throw flowers onto my grave; he was standing in it. I watched him closely as he slowly made his way up to the casket, careful not to lift his head high enough that someone might realize they did not recognize him. Once he was there, he carefully placed something small on top of it. It was small enough to fall through the flowers but made a soft clunk when it hit the hard surface. He then proceeded to walk away quickly, but steadily enough so as not to attract attention. He made his way back to his car without anyone noticing his presence there at all. I was completely stunned. How had no one noticed?

The camera then zoomed in on my casket so that I could see what he had left behind, and to my utter dismay, it was my ring. The one my mom had gotten for me when my father died. Solid gold, made from his wedding band melted down and turned into a beautiful rose-patterned ring. She gave it to me and not my sister because she knew how close my dad and I were and how much it hurt me when he had passed. She even told me the day she gave it to me, "Here baby, you need this more than I do." I will remember that line for as long as I am Carol.

By this point my tears had dried, creating pool-sized stains on my shirt, and my jaw had been dangling open long enough that I was thirsty. I just could not wrap my head around why he had given me back what was an expensive ring when he could have easily pawned it for money. As I stared, fixated at what I was seeing, I began to examine his car; it looked familiar. It was a black sedan, nothing out of the ordinary, but I couldn't help but feel attached to it, eerily drawn in. I needed to see it—the screen image was not budging, so I knew something was up, but what was I missing?

I closed my eyes to clear my head and focus. I looked at every detail—maybe a dent or a ding of some sort would jog my memory—but nothing stood out. Then I thought, *Maybe the intent is for me to remember it in case I see it later.* I tried to memorize the make and model; that was easy enough since I had the same car in red when I was alive. That is when I saw it: As he opened the door, I saw the sticker I had placed on the dash. The little "I Voted" flag sticker that had superglued itself to my dash so I could never get it off without making a mess. He was using *my* car still! I was furious! He had changed the paint color and was using my car! How could he? How could I have been so dense? Just when I was beginning to think he was remorseful for what he had done, I saw this! The ring was nothing in comparison to stealing my car! The murderous thief! But why take one and not the other?

I was getting so many mixed signals my head was spinning! I couldn't even talk straight; it all came out as a mumbling, muttering mess. I damn near spit I was so angry! I stomped my foot at every thought. How could this have happened to me? How did I get mixed up in this infuriating mess? I could do nothing but stand back and be angry; what had occurred felt like a box-ing match with my hands tied behind my back while my opponent went in for the cheap shots.

"Why?" I screamed. "I don't understand any of this! Why would he waste half his day and yet flamboyantly show he was using my own friggin' car? I can't stand it!"

"Calm down, Carol, this part is almost over," Gabe said in his usual soothing voice while gently rubbing my shoulders to try and ease my tension. It was a nice ges-ture, but I threw him off. I was too livid to even stand still long enough for that to be effective.

"Are you kidding me! There is more?" I said with a start. My face was already red, my mouth was dry, and my head was pounding from all the tears! I didn't know how much more I could endure, to be honest.

"Just be patient; it is almost through," he said in the same soothing, levelheaded tone. I couldn't help but scowl at him as if it were all his fault.

As he said this, the screen went back to the graveside, now empty except for my mother and sister. They were talking to an older gentleman, who I assumed worked there based on his attire and demeanor. He asked them, "Now, I know this is a very sensitive subject, but I need to ask; for that I am sorry. Would you like us to bury the empty casket with the items on top or would you like the grave to remain open until they are able to find the body?"

My sister looked at my mother, and they both said in unison, "Bury the casket."

Then my sister said with a quiver in her lip, "The police feel it necessary for us to seek closure since they do not feel they will ever find her remains." With my mother leaning on her, she slowly made her way back to her own car, softly comforting Mom. That is when the screen went black.

I did not realize it, but I had dropped to my knees. This was all so horrific I could not bear to stand any longer. What I had just been shown did not answer questions; it made me ask more. Why was he there? Have they found my body yet? If they did not have my body, how did they know I was dead? Why did he give back my ring but keep my car? Why did he even need to kill me? Was it on purpose or by accident? Where is the guy he was with? Where is the kid they had? Where is that kid's mom, the woman he was screaming for? It was impossible to get any sense of clarity or sense of direction after seeing the screen. Though it was meant to help me, it definitely left me with an uncertainty as to why I was even here. What could I possibly gain by this knowledge?

My sister and my mother sought closure; they did not have the means to continue the search for my remains, and with the audacity of my killer in showing up to my funeral, I doubt anyone other than he truly knew what had happened that morning or in the following days. The only trail I could follow was his. I needed to find out where he was going to figure out what he had done in the past, and, more importantly at this point, why. So I turned to Gabe with a resolute voice. "Show me how to find him."

"Ah, good choice. But you need to find out who he is before you can find out where he is now."

"If I knew who he was, I would probably not need to be teased and tainted with the miniseries of my life," I snapped back.

"That is not what I mean, Carol; I mean you need to find out his name. Once you have his name, you can seek out his record in the hall of records. This part may also take some digging, as it holds records of every living soul ever to exist on Earth, but it will have information on everything they have ever done, as well as everything they will ever do, until they come here."

"Ok. So I need to find his name, so I can find his

record and figure out what he did to me and, hopefully, what he did to the boy, right?"

"Well, hopefully yes."

"What do you mean 'hopefully'?"

"Carol, think back. Didn't you say there were two men? Where has the second man disappeared to? Was he as essential in your murder as that man was? Did they seem as if they were partners? What happened to this other man?"

"As much as I don't want to admit it, you are right. I don't know a thing about the first man, and even less about the other man who was there that day, as well as at the house. Now I don't know what to do—do I hunt down the guy I have been seeing on the screen or do I seek out the other man? You just made a complicated and frustrating situation even more complicated and frustrating—thanks."

"I can't tell you whom to seek first; I can only be here to guide you."

"Come again?" I said in a huffed voice. "How can you not answer that? I thought you were my caretaker, showing me what to do and all?"

"No, honey," he said sweetly to calm me down. "I am here to guide you through. I do not ever presume to show you what you must do unless I am instructed to do so."

I gave him a blank, dumbfounded stare, and it took me a few minutes to gather the right questions to ask. "Ok. So if you cannot tell me what to do and can only guide me, where do you recommend I start my search for the man on the screen? Since he is the one I know the most about, though I don't know much at all, he should be able to lead me both to the other man and the boy, as well as to the place where my own remains are."

"That is a brilliant place to start, my dear. I suggest you seek out"—he paused for a minute—"your father."

With all the new information fluttering in my brain—and now the thought of being able to see my father again—my knees wobbled and gave out beneath me. As I toppled to the floor, I caught a glimpse of Gabe darting to catch me, but it was too late. I felt my body hit the ground like a ton of bricks, and out I went.

CHAPTER 7

As I woke up to the birds chirping outside my window, I knew I needed to get a move on it. I didn't have time to dwell on the annoying, recurring theme of my waking up in a place I did not fall asleep in. I needed to see my father—not just to learn about that coward that killed me but also to be able to see him again, something I had been longing for since he passed all those years ago. I had had no idea I might have that ability, as I had been so consumed with myself that I did not consider those who had passed before me. I damn near flew into the closet and in a flash changed into something lightweight; I needed something I felt comfortable running in. I was out in the kitchen for my morning cup of coffee, which, instead of savoring, I planned to guzzle down before heading out the door. "Woman on a mission here; get out of my way," I said aloud as if someone cared. I didn't know which way I was going, but I knew I was headed somewhere and that someone would find me to guide my way. I grabbed my cup of coffee, spun around to lean on the counter so as not to spill all over myself, and saw Gabe lazily strewn across the armchair with one leg stretched over the arm and his body sprawled the full length of the chair. With his usual apple in hand and mouth full, he said almost sarcastically, "So are you ready to go?"

Coffee came spewing out of my mouth, all down my chin, all over the front of my clothes, and all over the floor. I was furious as I gagged and began to heave up lava-hot coffee from my lungs and out of my nose.

"Every time! You can't even spare me once with a knock at the door? You just let yourself in and get comfortable? You didn't even make a sound! How long were you even here? I am getting that bell to put around your neck; this is getting ridiculous—you even ruined this shirt…" I trailed off as I tried to clean myself up.

"Yikes, Carol, calm down," he said at my side, stroking my arm to comfort me. "I didn't realize you would have such a flair for the dramatic."

"It's not dramatic! It's courtesy. I don't like getting popped in on, and from the looks of it, that is your preferred method of saying hello!"

"That's nonsense. Now, moving on, are you ready to see your father?" he said, completely changing the subject.

After my vision cleared, I reached for my new, fresh coffee, which was waiting for me on the counter. Took a few sips to clear my head then said, "Yup, I'm ready to go." I was trying not to shoot daggers out of my eyes.

He smiled at me, took my hand, and headed for

the door. Once outside we could see the two roads, one headed toward the library and the other toward the ruins and the mountains. As we stood there, Gabe told me something very important. "Now this is something you will need to know for later on. Not every path here has a road. The people you seek, you will find, but you will need to search for them. You will be guided by the collective intelligence that is throughout heaven. This will give you the intuitive ability to find the person you seek. Does this make sense?"

It took me a few minutes to process. "Umm, I guess. So you are basically telling me to go wander, that I will find what I need to find?"

"Precisely."

"Ok then. Off we go, I guess," I said as we headed off the porch and into the front yard. We walked to the end of the grass where it met the now-forked path. Instead of turning right or left, I decided to go straight through the meadow. With me uneasily glancing at Gabe for reassurance, we continued through the meadow. The brush grew deeper and deeper as we continued; it topped off at around four feet. I didn't want to show how uncertain I was with this decision; maybe it was not so far off the original path? I felt my anxiety level skyrocket once I glanced over my shoulder and could not see my home anymore.

"You are doing fine, I promise. I am here to guide you, remember? Just remember what you are trying to find and be certain of it; it will come."

This calmed me until we reached the end of the

meadow and headed into a wooded area. It seemed relatively peaceful, but the vegetation grew thicker and thicker the deeper we wandered in. The trees had created such a canopy it was hard to see in front of us. Gabe and I both had tripped over overgrown plants and uprooted trees. This started to scare me; my heart began pounding faster, and my thoughts strayed into my doubts.

This is when Gabe slowly took my hand in his own. "We are in this together—clear your thoughts and refocus on your intention. We can do this as long as you are certain you can."

With that I stopped dead in my tracks and closed my eyes. I couldn't very well clear my head when trying constantly not to trip over everything. I thought of all the warm memories of my father and how I missed him daily. I remembered his smile and our little trips to get ice cream after dinner. I remembered his laugh and how angry he would get if his favorite football team was slacking in the last quarter. A smile crept across my face; all the while I held onto Gabe's hand. When I opened my eyes, I could see the same smile on Gabe's face. "He looks like a wonderful father."

"He was," I said sincerely. "He knew how to bring me up when I was down." As I said this, I glanced down and saw a very faint path etched into the woods. "Look!" I said. "Has this been here this whole time?"

"No, ma'am. This path was created by you; you cleared the path as you cleared your cluttered thoughts. Keep true and we should make it soon."

I was elated; hand in hand Gabe and I made our way down the faint but distinguishable path through the woods and out into a clearing by a crystal-clear lake. It shimmered in the sunlight and was perfectly manicured, as if it were straight out of a portrait, so much so it I gave me a vague sense of familiarity. To the right was a small home with wisps of smoke coming out of its chimney. It was white with an earth-toned stone façade. The path leading up to the front door was river rock, to match the lake house feel. The cool breeze coming off the lake brought up rich, woodsy smells mixed with the aroma of a freshwater spring. Not your usual dead fish smell, like some of the Earth's lakes have.

"Is that his house?"

"You know the answer to that, Carol," he said as he gently nudged me forward. We walked the rest of the way to the front door in silence.

Standing in the doorway, too nervous to knock, I felt like we looked ridiculous. Like two small children trying to sell cookies to a neighbor—uncomfortable, nervous, and slightly scared of what we would find on the other side of the door. We were standing on a small wooden porch next to a single rocker chair with a big, fluffy pillow, still holding its shape but obviously well worn, based on the fade in the flannel pattern. My heart was beating at double speed, and my palms were sweating; I could not stop fidgeting. After a few minutes, Gabe's voice startled me out of my trance. "Carol, what are you waiting for?" he said soothingly. "Isn't this what you wanted?"

Stumbling over myself, I said, "Well, uh, yeah...but um, he, well...it's hard, ok?" I said, nearly shouting. After I said that, I heard footsteps. It was my father; he had heard me talking to Gabe on his front porch. He was headed for the door; I could hear him getting closer with every thud. I began to panic. I wasn't sure I could handle this; I wanted to run. I turned to dart from the porch and back into the woods, where I ironically felt safe, but Gabe had a hold on my hand. He had never let it go; this time he clasped both of his hands over mine and without words began stroking my hand to calm me down. I felt more at ease staring into his bright blue eyes. I had never noticed how deep they went; they were almost as calm and blue as the water of the lake. He took a deep breath, and I followed his lead and slowed my breathing to match his own just as the door swung open.

There he was, all six-foot-two of him, standing in front of me just as I remembered him in his glory days—his hair was no longer white but caramel, and even his beard didn't show any signs of aging. He was a large man, thick but fit; even death had not stopped him from chopping and stacking his own wood. When I looked at his face, it was as if I could see my own; I carried so many of his features, from his squared chin to his almond eyes and longer nose. Now, we aren't talking a Pinocchio nose or anything—good size for Midwestern living, probably room for concern on the West coast, but my mind wanders. I stared into his big brown eyes and started to sob. Even he couldn't hold back the tears when he saw me.

I ran into his arms as if I were still a small child and he was there to mend all my boo-boos, and he didn't hesitate to run to me as well. As we stood in a deep embrace, I could not help but feel as if I were at home again. His arms were so warm and comforting, and even with us both sobbing, we knew they were happy tears, a reflection of finally being with each other again.

"My baby girl, I have been waiting for you."

"I know, Daddy; I have missed you for so long!"

"I missed you too, honey. As much as I wanted to see you and your mother and sister, I knew I needed to wait for you all to come to me. I didn't expect to see you this soon, though," he said with a twinge of sadness.

"Daddy," I said through tears. I tried to dry them, but every time I laid eyes on him, more took the place of the ones I had just wiped away, creating a steady stream no matter how hard I tried. "I am not here because I died of old age, I was"—I stammered again—"I was…" I couldn't even muster the words. The subject was still too painful to bring up. I had not realized talking about it would be so painful; I barely knew any of the details that would make it painful!

"You were murdered, my baby girl; I know," he said as he stroked my hair, something he would do to calm me as a kid during storms or if I had nightmares.

"Yes!" I inadvertently shouted. I hated hearing it; it made me feel so helpless, as if I were branded for the rest of my days as someone victimized. It was as if I were a weakling in life easily overtaken, when in fact I felt the complete opposite. I had made myself into a strong and independent woman; I did not need to feel less than that. The worst part was it was all in my own head. No one had made me feel inferior but myself.

"I know, I know. It's ok now; look at me," he said as he lifted my chin. "Look at me; have I ever steered you wrong?"

I managed a small laugh. "No."

"And you know, Carol, that time on your bicycle when you were five, which you can never seem to forget, does *not* count," he said with a sly grin on his face.

I burst out laughing, which made him burst out laughing. He had always known how to get a hysterically crying female to calm down; he did, after all, have a wife and two daughters. After ten solid minutes of embracing me, my dad, whom I had missed so dearly, said, "Well, don't you just stand there, come on in."

I turned to summon Gabe into the house behind me, only to find that he had disappeared on me—again. "Well, I was going to have Gabe come in as well, but I guess not."

"Gabe is a very busy guy, baby girl. I am sure he knew that he left you in good hands."

A little puzzled, I said, "You know who Gabe is?"

"Well, I know he is your caretaker, and he has visited me before." Then he paused for a slight second. "And he is a little bit famous up here."

Not sure which one was more important to round back to, I said, "Wait, he visited you? I know he had others, but I thought he said they had to be special cases. Famous? How so?"

"Calm down, baby girl; he came to visit me once. It was for a very specific purpose—"

"Which is?" I interjected.

"Honey, he came to me after I was shown what happened to you—not exactly what a father wants to see. I knew something was wrong when this showed up on my nightstand that morning. I didn't understand it until he appeared at my door; you know how they only like to give you bits and pieces. What I had been shown, coupled with this, left me so confused I walked into the door trying to answer it for Gabe. He sat me down, and the screen popped on, showing me the details. He said you would be coming to see me when you were ready, that I should remember everything that was shown so I can help you when the time comes." As he was telling me this, he reached into his pocket and pulled out something small and shiny. He opened his palm to reveal the gold ring I always wore, the one my killer had put back on my grave before he had driven off in *my* car. I took it from his hand and rubbed it gently between my fingers. Seeing the ring started the tears flowing—it was something so simple yet tangible. I didn't realize how much I would miss the physical items I had when I was alive.

"How did this make its way back to you?" I sniffled as I handed it back to him it. Once the ring touched his hand it began to mutate; the change startled us both. I gasped, and simultaneously he jumped, dropping the ring to the ground. We almost butted heads trying to get a closer look at the ring; it had completely transformed back into its original form, his wedding band.

With a tear streaming down his face, he picked up the band and slipped it onto his left ring finger.

"Right back where you belong," he said with a sniffle. He looked me in the eyes. "They say if you were fortunate enough in life to be with your true love, they will come back to you after you have passed from Earth. I guess this ring brought us back together; it gives me hope I will see your mother and sister again."

"I hope so too. I want them to know I am ok—actually, that we are both ok and they don't need to worry."

"Especially about you, Carol. They know how I passed; it was early but not out of the ordinary. You, on the other hand...Come inside; we will talk."

My dad guided me through the door into his small home. Comfort and safety encompassed me as we entered—something I could only feel with him, something I had only ever felt with him. I had never met a man that could make me feel as comfortable in my own skin and as loved as he could with a single smile.

"You don't need a whole lot up here, if you haven't noticed. I am perfectly happy with just the view and a soft place to sleep," he was saying as we walked through his small home. There was a little living area, which contained a long, deep couch that took up half the room, and the other side was all windows. A small end table with a lamp fashioned crudely of wood—just looking at it gave me the sharp, familiar sting of a splinter. The floor was a nice cherrywood with a large oriental area rug. Very plain walls—not a single thing hung from them. From the entrance you could see into his bedroom, which looked similar: the same red-brown-white color scheme and very plain. I guess you could call it rustic or masculine; it definitely lacked a feminine touch. I would not have expected anything fancy from him. He was never the type to complain, always happy with what he was given.

I began to notice exactly how small the house really was; there were some very specific rooms missing. "Where are your bathroom and kitchen?" I asked as I poked my nose into every corner.

"No need for that anymore. I had them for a while and realized the food I always wanted just appeared on the end table, so I never bothered going into the kitchen. I never went into the bathroom either, so both rooms just disappeared. I didn't notice for the longest time, until one day I went looking for something I could have sworn I had here and realized there were rooms completely gone. The hall closet too—there were sheets and towels in there, but the whole thing is gone. Ha ha. I guess the big guy upstairs knew I wasn't about to do laundry! Ha!"

"Disappeared? Very Interesting. I will need to check that out when I get back to my home. Come to think of it, I do remember you asking me how to turn on the washing machine a few years before you died. I guess Mom spoiled you in that way, huh, Pops?" I giggled.

"Go check it out; I bet the areas you thought you needed but never used are either not there or drastically smaller than the last time you checked." Then with a sigh, he said, "Yes, your saint of a mother did spoil me. That's why I miss her to this day."

"I will definitely take a look around, and I miss them too."

He and I went on and on for hours just reminiscing about old memories and talking about his transition. Since his passing had been far less traumatic, his only tasks were to relax and be there for the few that would need his help. His caretaker visited him seldomly and usually didn't even stay long enough to finish a conversation. He couldn't even recall her name when I asked. It became a little joke between us.

"In fact, Carol, I kid you not, one day I turned back to take a seat on the couch, and before by butt even hit the cushion, she was gone!" He and I burst out laughing at the thought. "I think I actually had a longer conversation with Gabe than I have ever had with my own caretaker. Can we switch?" He joked and started to crack up again. Clearing his throat and taking on a more serious tone, he continued, "Gabe is a nice guy, very intuitive; you can tell why he was put on your case." It was as if the thought of Gabe had brought Dad's thoughts to a screeching halt with the realization that I had been allowed to see him with a specific purpose in mind.

"Yeah, I know, because it was so horrific, right?"

"Well, yes, that and how dramatic you can be—"

"*Dad!* What do you mean 'dramatic'? I was killed; how can you not be 'dramatic' about that!"

"Well, honey, how do I put this…" He hesitated, looking to choose his words wisely. "You just have a tendency to overreact"

"Not always. I have gotten better," I said, gritting my

teeth. I couldn't let him be right about this one. The conversation alone made me feel like I was a little kid again.

"Gabe says you are a fainter," he said with a grin on his face.

"What? Is there no confidentiality around here?" My face had turned bright red with embarrassment.

"Nope. Everyone knows everything when you move up."

"Fine. I guess I will need to get better about that, but it's not easy when you are shown the things he has shown me."

Soothingly he said, "I understand; now have a seat. I know what you are itching to find out about—and no fainting on me, remember?" He said with a chuckle to ease my stress.

I plopped down on his big, brown, comfortable couch; you could tell it was well used, but it did not bear any signs of wear. I nestled in like a child eager for their bedtime story. My dad sat himself on the other end and faced me, fidgeting to get comfortable. We looked at each other for a moment, I think just to soak in the fact that the other was truly there, in the flesh. Well, as fleshy as one could get in this side. With not a word spoken between us, he reached for my hand. He held it gently in his own and gave it a few pats. "I know what happened to you was definitely not something you would ever expect to happen, but it did."

I nodded my head along as he went into further detail; just those few words were already making me emotional. "From what I saw when you were taken, the men grabbed you after you hit the ground and put you into the trunk of your own car. The passenger in the car, who stood by as you were hit over the head, grabbed the little boy from their back seat and shoved him in the back seat of your car. They then hurriedly grabbed a couple of things before bashing in the windows and throwing the keys into the nearby woods." He slowed down, as if it had become painful for him to tell me, as he watched the steady stream of tears rolling down my cheeks. I had to encourage him to continue with a faint head nod and quivering smile. "As the screen continued to show me, the main driver, who seemed to be the leader, in my opinion, and the other guy, whatever he was, talked the whole way to the house. They eventually threw you into the shed." He sped up after saying that, as if in effort to skirt the issue. "Now, while they were talking, I could only understand a little bit of what they were saying. They were speaking to each other in a foreign language, one that was difficult for me to understand, but there were a few words I caught."

"Wait, I thought up here you would be able to understand all languages as one? And"—I grabbed and squeezed his hand—"I know they kept my body in a shed; what happened after that I do not know, but that much I know."

"That's a relief. Not what happened to you, but I dreaded the idea of having to be the one to tell you about that horrific shed. The language thing—not until you transition. There are some things you will be able to pick out if you truly try, but not until you transition to the next level of heaven will you know and understand every language as one universal language."

"Well, crap," I muttered.

"I know. I know. Just be patient—what I could understand may be able to help you. The sidekick, let's call him, asked the driver about the house; from what I could tell, he had never seen it before. This I thought was odd. Anyway, they continued to talk; all I could catch was a reference to Mason, which I assumed was about the little boy knocked out in the back seat, and one other name—Madison. They said them together, but I wish I could understand why. I could really only assume the worst. So remember those names, baby girl, because I heard them for a reason. That is one thing you will learn up here—everything happens for a reason. Things are not random; this is something on Earth I always neglected to notice, and now I wish I had, because it is universal."

"Mason and Madison? I definitely can't remember any girl with them; I wonder who Madison is, or was? Wait, you said on Earth it was the same way? Nothing random?"

"Nope, nothing was random. People, things, feelings—they were all there for a reason. When you got the chills from someone, that was for a reason. When you saw signs for something over and over again, that was there to tell you something. There may not have been divine intervention, as some would think or desperately cling to hope for, but there is a master plan, and everyone and everything fits perfectly into it for a reason. Take, for example, my death."

"Dad, you died of a heart attack; how did signs have anything to do with that?"

"Honey, toward my last days, I remember ignoring all sorts of signs, things as mundane as excessive heart attack references on TV to sharp pains and tingling. Nothing is random; had I been more intuitive, I would have gone to the doctor or asked for help. That could have bought me at least a couple more years with my girls."

"But if everything is predestined, you were meant to die when you did, right?"

"Yes and no. You are born, you are destined to live, and you are destined to die, usually in a specific way. Some people, if they are intuitive enough, can buy themselves time, but to be human is to have finite days to your existence. From the day every baby is born, it is a countdown to their predestined death."

"That's ridiculously morbid," I said with a shudder.

"It is, but it is not—that is why life is so precious and needs to be lived to its fullest. What is morbid is to think of how many there are out there who lived a miserable and short existence and could truly not enjoy their time. Granted, getting here isn't so bad, but when you realize the things you have taken for granted back on Earth, you will understand why the final transition is back to Earth for another round."

I looked at him thoughtfully. "Are you close to transitioning yourself, Dad?"

Without hesitation, he said, "No. I am waiting for your mother to join me. We will transition together, if that is permitted."

I loved hearing him say that. It was heartwarming and so deeply satisfying to know that love like theirs truly did exist in life. It was something I wish I had seen more of in my life back on Earth.

"I digress." He continued. "So the names I heard were Mason and Madison. They then continued talking in their own native language, and the little boy began to stir, which caused the second man to panic. When he started panicking, the driver said, 'Aaron, calm down; if he wakes up, just scare him straight.' This I heard clear as crystal."

"Aaron? The second guy did not look like an Aaron from what I can remember. I know this sounds bad, but he was way too tan to be an Aaron."

"I thought the same thing. He did not look like one at all, but I'm not done either. After the driver said that to Aaron, he did get upset as expected and retorted with 'Ali, you act like it is so easy!' They began to argue in their language, and then the screen changed. It had definitely shown me the car ride to reveal their names. I can tell you that much because it was the only part I could really understand."

He continued, and I was completely enthralled with what he was telling me. It was as if the entire room around us had completely vanished and I was living through exactly what he had seen. Well, technically I was there—but that's not really the point. "When the screen changed, they were in the car still, but they had stopped. I was able to see the gas station sign from the reflection in the rearview mirror. The men had calmed down after their argument, and the little boy was awake now. He seemed petrified and was curled up in the corner behind the driver. The child looked like he was trying to stay as small as he could, as if this would make him small enough to disappear altogether. Ali kept looking around and then lifted his whole body in the air and reached for his wallet, which was in his back pocket; he maneuvered it out and opened it up to see how much cash he had. He flipped through and had a couple of singles but not enough for what he needed—that much I could read off his facial expressions. He then turned the wallet and proceeded to take out a credit card; he hesitated, clearly knowing this could leave a trail, and in his hesitation, I was able to catch the name on the credit card. His name is Ali Garcia."

Relieved to have a name to start with and still getting a sickening, sinking feeling in my stomach, I tried to remain in control, especially because my dad was sitting across from me. He had always been so strong for me; it was my turn to show him what I was made of, especially knowing that Gabe had blabbed about my uncanny ability to lose consciousness when overwhelmed. I sucked it up and, acting unscathed, said, "That will definitely help me. Gabe was saying there is record of every soul in the library; have you been?'

"Yes. When I feel lonely or want to know how you girls are doing, I check out your records in the library. I know you will all eventually make it here, but it's not the same as knowing how you have turned out in life and all the things I had to miss."

Saddened by the grieved expression on his face, I said, "Have you checked on us a lot?"

"You tell me? Have you felt my presence around you a lot since I have been gone?"

"Yes. Not at first, but there were definitely times I felt you with me; I would feel my hair stand on end when I reflected on it. I thought I was crazy, but I swear I could smell your cologne some days. Was that actually you?"

"Yes, that was me. One of the things they tell you when you check out someone's record is that they may feel you watching them or feel you are with them. This is a double-edged sword because you may end up scaring the ones you love unintentionally."

"Oh, I will definitely keep that in mind. Thank you, Dad," I said as I gave him a huge hug, not wanting to let go. "Will I be able to come back and visit you?"

"You certainly will," he said as he was walking me to the door. "Baby girl, I know you are in a hurry to understand everything—you have always been that way—but I need you to slow down a little on this one. You may do more harm than good to yourself if you push too hard too fast."

"Why would I do that? I know his name; now I just need to figure out why he did it, where he is now, and what he did with the little boy—and little girl."

"Honey, think about it. We know the name on the credit card; based off his actions, do you really think he is using his real name? Do you really feel it will be that easy? Remember, the monsters in life are always based off humans; they make the worst beasts. They are the ones that can hurt you more deeply than any animal ever created or imagined."

With a pause and a slight chill running up my spine, I knew I had to push through his warning. I would not be able to continue without finding out as soon as possible; I could not bear the anxiety anymore. "I hope that is the name. It is the only lead I have. I need to start somewhere; I am hoping this takes me to where I need to be. I love you, Dad, and I will try to be as cautious as I can with this, but you know me," I said with a growing grin creeping across my face.

"For your sake, I hope so too, baby girl," he said as he hugged me again and ushered me out the door. "I will see you soon, yes?"

"Of course you will. Now that I know how to find you, I will be able to come back here whenever I need you." I left him on the porch with one of the biggest smiles I had ever seen from him. I began walking back toward the woods as I ran all these images and scenarios over in my mind. Before I realized it, I was surrounded by woods and at a dead stop. Every direction I turned, I was engulfed in trees and foliage. I felt my chest tighten as I began to panic at my carelessness. After a few minutes of panic, I calmed myself enough to follow one coherent thought and tried to remember what Gabe had told me.

"What was that thing he was telling me?" I said out loud to myself. "Something like, the harder you focus on something, the clearer the path becomes?" It was worth a shot; it was my only option! So I thought, *Home, home, home,* and opened my eyes. I had to search to see a small path cleared away through the trees. So I thought instead of fumbling around through the narrow pathway, I would do it again—close my eyes and concentrate on where I needed to be. If it worked for Dorothy, it should work for me. "There's no place like home, there's no place like home, there's no place like home." With a grin I opened my eyes and burst out laughing at the sight; apparently I wasn't the only one with a sense of humor! I opened my eyes to see a nicely laid out path of yellow brick winding through the trees and off into the distance. I was so thrilled I skipped down the path toward home, humming, "We're off to see the wizard…"

I was having a blast now that I wasn't lost anymore. Part of me didn't think it would happen, like it was some sort of blasphemy, but then I realized that the path leading to my home was yellow brick, so why couldn't this one be? After all, it is what I make it, right? I neared the end of the woods and saw the meadow that lay before my house. The path home was most certainly shorter than the path to my dad's place. I wondered if that was because I had lost my way. It was a neat trick I would certainly need to remember for the future. It would come in handy someday.

I got to the front porch just as the sun was about to set. I eased myself into my chair and watched the sun as it finally disappeared under the horizon. It was just as beautiful as the sunrise had been; it warmed me with its dying glow. With a sigh I dragged my worn feet inside, straight into the kitchen, and grabbed the chicken pot pie from the microwave. I was salivating at the sight—it looked just like the ones my mom used to make when I was a kid. I devoured it within minutes and dragged myself off to bed like a tiger after a large feeding. It took only a few blinks before I was out like a light from exhaustion.

CHAPTER 8

I opened my eyes to the morning sunlight streaming in through the window. It felt as if I had slept for a month, but instead of having those slept-too-long-in-bed pains, I awoke refreshed and revived, ready for a new adventure. I popped out of bed and stretched. I looked over toward the bathroom and remembered what my dad had said. I walked in to see everything the way I remembered it, but oddly enough it seemed a little bit smaller. I said out loud, "That's strange; I wonder if that is just me or if it truly is smaller than it was?" I opened the top drawer on the vanity, and it was empty. "Umm, where did my brush go?" So then I searched more drawers. I grabbed at the chrome handles and pulled, but they didn't budge. "What the heck!"

I swung around and was face-to-face with the towel cabinet. I pulled on the handle and was surprised that it opened. I swung it wide open and saw nothing. Absolutely nothing. Not one single towel, not one single string. "He was right; I only come in here to look in the mirror after

I get dressed. I don't even shower anymore because there isn't anything that gets me dirty; I don't even sweat anymore!" I even walked around and looked into the shower, and there wasn't a single thing in there. So I tested the water, and the handles didn't even turn! So I tried the toilet, and same thing! "This is all here, but for show. I can't believe it!" Good thing I never had to pass a bowel movement; that would have been a mess waiting to happen!

I walked out of the bathroom, giggling at the sight of it all, and sat at the edge of my bed; I took a long look around the room to see if anything else was missing or different. Then I remembered my closet! I went into the closet and realized most of the things I thought were in the back of the closet were now completely gone—including that part of the closet! It was half the size it used to be. So then I wandered through the house and looked at the dining room, where, instead of a grand table, there was now a small, four-seat table with flowers on it. I was completely shocked. "*How* did I miss that! I walk by this damn thing every day! Ha!" I kept walking and went into the kitchen. "Now I know if bathroom stuff is gone, kitchen stuff is gone too." I opened every cabinet that would open and found nothing—not a cup or saucer or plate in sight. I looked for small appliances—all gone too. "This is freaky." A little disturbed, I went back into the bedroom and sat on my bed again. "At least this isn't gone." I laughed to myself. I looked over at my nightstand and stared at the frame for a few minutes; I then realized it, too, had been an oddity. It had been there this whole time, and I had never once given any thought as to who was in the picture. "Who are these girls," I couldn't help but ponder. "I thought they were younger than this," I said as I looked closely at the picture still worn around the edges. The girls looked so familiar, yet I had no idea who they were. But now they looked somehow older, no longer little six- and eight-year-old-looking babies, but closer to eight- and ten-year-old-looking kids. "Who are you?" I muttered.

"You will see," Gabe said as he leaned against the doorframe in my bedroom, eating yet another apple. From fright I almost dropped the picture—I fumbled it from hand to hand before it came inches from hitting the ground, but I managed to catch it.

"Seriously? A bell! I will put a bell on you!"

"Now why would you do a thing like that?" He laughed.

"To keep you from killing me!" He gave me the funniest look as I realized what I had said. "You know exactly what I mean."

"No, actually I don't; see, I never was on Earth. I believe I may have told you this before," he said in his smug, vaguely sarcastic way.

"Probably," I said awkwardly. There was a moment of silence as he chomped away on the apple, staring at me all the while. "So anyway, why are you here?"

Completely unfazed by the awkward silence, he said, "I am here because you are ready for your search in the records."

"I need help to search for a name?" I asked sarcastically.

"Well, it may be difficult since the records encompass any living soul throughout time who held a given name."

"I see. Well, I guess we should get started then, huh?"

"Yes, ma'am; right this way." He held open my front door for me. We headed out the door in the direction of the library and took the walk at a nice, leisurely pace. Not a word was spoken between us for a vast leg of the journey until I broke the silence out of sheer boredom.

"So do you think I have completed the most difficult aspect of my journey?"

He looked at me with a blank look; he seemed extremely distracted and slightly dumbfounded at my question. "Well, some of it, yes. Your journey is unlike most others'. Most cases are more straightforward; yours will need a bit more digging."

"Is it because of the two men?"

Exasperated, he said, "Carol, this is your journey. I can only guide you; I cannot offer you more information. As much as I would love to tell you everything you need to know, this is all part of his master plan," he said as he pointed upward.

"So you are telling me you know exactly what happened? To me? To the little boy? You know what my dad was going to tell me and what I will find out next? You have known everything this whole time and have been sitting around watching me struggle with this?"

We continued forward for a minute without a response from Gabe.

"Hello? Anyone with me?" I said as I waved my hand

in front of his distracted face, growing more furious at the idea he was holding out on me when I could easily have been in a position to move on instead of constantly struggling with the unchangeable past.

"Yes, Carol," he finally said with irritation in his voice. "I know what is to come, and no, I cannot help you with any of that information. I know this may cause you unnecessary frustration, but this is *your* journey, not mine. It is not for me to tell you."

I changed the subject since he clearly was becoming more distraught from the questioning. "Why are you so distracted, anyway? More so than usual."

"Sorry for that. I do not want to neglect anyone while I am with them; I have just been given more orders from above. These have a tendency to distract me."

This piqued my curiosity. "Oh, I see. So let me ask you something. Do you have to work for all eternity? Is there any rest for you?"

"I have been designed to be a caretaker, yes. Not all souls go down to Earth; some stay up here. There are also some souls that decide not to transition back to Earth, and they can make the decision to stay where they are or pursue a more meaningful existence and become a caretaker as well."

"Oh, I'm sorry. Do you know what people decide before they pull the trigger, so to speak?"

"No. After you have reached heaven, you know things about the past and future, but that is one thing you do not know. You can predict most things but not what is in someone's heart—only what is in someone's head. That decision is made by the heart, something untouchable."

We approached the library entrance. It was still a feast for the eyes to see—all the animals and souls alike living in harmony. Completely breathtaking how the light glistened off the stone façade, making the whole structure come alive. It reminded me of a bright college campus, full of energy and hope, but this place was so much more, so much more alive in its own ironic way. We walked through the grand entrance; I needed to remind myself to breathe! From this point Gabe needed to guide me, partially so I wouldn't walk into a pillar and partially because I had no clue where to start. We walked from the entrance in a straight line toward the back of the building, passing all the occupied rooms, with some souls deep in thought with their noses buried in books, others seemingly meditating, and a great number glued to screens.

"We are heading back to the hall of records," he said as we passed what seemed like a mile of shelves full of books in the blink of an eye. He then veered to the left and through a narrowing hallway. We came to the entrance; a large, aging sign over the rounded doorframe stated HALL OF RECORDS.

It looked so formal, as if it were a government office. The whole tone had changed; the souls in this room were definitely searching for someone. Some were in a frantic search, while others searched more methodically and calmly. As more souls approached the room, you could tell who the frequent visitors were by how quickly and quietly they were able to find their files, with almost a sixth sense about it. Others, who were with their caretakers, looked like deer in the headlights—what I could only imagine I looked like! The room itself was not as majestic as I had expected it to be. It looked like it was miles in length, with tall, metal, beige filing shelves, one after the other, that took up three-fourths of the width of the room. The walls were stark white, and there were small desk stations located at the end of each shelving unit. It was quiet, so much more so than the rest of the library. Deafening almost. Saying you could have heard a pin drop would have been an understatement.

I'm sure, based off my expression, that Gabe could tell I was beginning to become stressed out. He gave me a look and took my hand so I knew he was there to help. He said quietly, "This is the hard part—finding the correct file. The contents of this room are organized chronologically and alphabetically. You will need to find the correct year of birth and search by last name."

"Year of birth?" I said, discouraged.

"Yes, and since you don't know his year of birth, you will need to start somewhere, either the oldest you think he could be or the youngest, and work your way back. This will be time-consuming and challenging, and no, there is not an easier way. How would you like to start?"

As I more closely looked at each of the shelving units, I now noticed years written on the sides; the records dated back to 10,000 BC. A head-spinning number!

"It is dated this way because it became too confusing for people to understand the real dates, so it was all switched over long ago in a way more souls could understand."

"Ah, I see," I said, trying not to seem dumb, though I knew he could see straight through me. "So I guess I will start with the youngest he could possibly be. Based on what I remember, there was no way he was under twenty-seven, so I will start with—well, let me do the basic math here. I died in 2016, and he would have been around twenty-seven, so…" I stammered since math was never my strongest subject.

"1989," Gabe said quickly.

"Yeah, of course, 1989; that's what I got too," I said, a little embarrassed that I couldn't figure that out in a reasonable amount of time.

"Don't mention it," he said with a sly grin.

"You know, you are getting a little sassier; am I rubbing off on you?" I smiled. Before he could respond, we were shushed by half a dozen souls searching the shelves around us. They were so quiet; it spooked me to know there were so many potentially listening to our conversation and, even more so, that they were close enough to touch us without me even knowing!

"Sorry," I whispered. I looked at Gabe, and he gave me a head nod to walk toward the back. I had to rub the goose bumps down from my arms as we silently walked toward the back, getting glared at by all the disrupted souls.

He whispered to me, "We may be walking a little while to get there, and it may be more congested at that end, so try and stay patient and not disturb more souls than we already have."

We continued toward the back of the room, walking by what felt like miles of endless and identical shelves. It was difficult to gauge how deep we were into the room. The only way to tell was by how small the souls at the entrance had become. By the time we reached the correct century, we saw more and more souls congesting the aisles and fewer and fewer souls near the entrance. We reached the shelving unit labeled *1989.*

"We are here," Gabe said. "Now this is where you begin to search. You will need to find the year and then his name. This may take you some time; some of the files are quite thick, while others are much smaller. You will see what I mean when you start pulling the files."

"Why is that? Because some die young while others live for a long time?"

"Yes and no. The files vary with every soul based on their actions in life. If they lived for a long time but did very little with their time on Earth, their file will be smaller than that of someone who lived half as long but lead a much fuller life—meaning, more notable moments to be filed."

"I guess that makes sense, but what would be considered 'notable'?"

"Notable as in life changing events, gaining more knowledge, affecting more lives, things of that nature; keep in mind that does not necessarily mean affecting lives in a positive way, as you will see with your killer. You will be in his file, but he obviously did not affect you in a positive way."

"Yeah, not so much," I muttered.

With a smile, he said, "Ok, Carol, this is where I believe you will be all right on your own. Good luck."

"Thanks," I said, a little puzzled. He had never said goodbye to me—usually he just disappeared—but this time he just walked away and slipped behind the shelves. "That was odd. Maybe I am finally growing on him," I said as a satisfied smile crept across my face. The smile lasted from *A* to *D* before I realized I still was grinning like a fool. I shook my head to get the smile off my face and so I could regain my focus on the task at hand. As I got closer to "Garcia," I became more and more anxious.

I turned the corner onto the next shelving unit, and there, right in my face, was "Garcia." My heart skipped a beat. I grabbed the corner of the unit to keep from losing balance. I scanned each of the names from Aaron all the way to Byron. "Crap! Time to move to the next year, I guess." I made my way through the end of the alphabet and back to the shelves of 1988. I did the same thing—found the section on "Garcia," grabbed the corner again (I didn't want to make the stumble to the floor unless I actually found his file), and searched from Aaron to Branson. "Damn, not here either."

I continued my search the same way with the same death grip on the shelves from 1989 to 1972 before starting to feel completely discouraged. Continuing my search from 1972 to 1968, I began to feel doomed and helpless. I thought to myself, *What did I do wrong? Why is this so hard?* He was supposed to be here. This was supposed to be the last piece of the puzzle, but it was not happening. I had reached my breaking point by the time I came to 1960. There was no way he was over fifty-five when he killed me. I was exhausted and needed a break. So I walked the miles of shame out of the hall of records and back into the main library. I looked around as I left and saw others as discouraged as I was, but mostly saw those who seemed content, with their heads held high and a slight pep in their step. I glared at those souls and moped on out of the library like a scolded dog with my tail between my legs. I was too annoyed and anxious to continue on that day. I needed to clear my head and start again the next day.

I made my way back home and knew that my journey would be at a standstill until I found this file. "There has to be something I am missing. I don't understand why his name is not there." Walking into my little home, I plopped on the couch and grabbed the nearest pillow I could find. I then buried my face in my pillow and *screamed* until I couldn't catch my breath. For the rest of the evening, I sat and stared at the bookshelves. I couldn't bring myself to move. I had to think clearly; what could I be missing? There has to be a file. Where was his file? I knew what I had to do—I needed to continue looking. Not an epiphany, but something I needed to conclude. I needed to find the answer. That was my only task, and it was already proving to be more difficult than I had expected.

CHAPTER 9

It was months of the same routine. I would wake up.
Drink my coffee. Walk to the library. Spend all day
in the hall of records. Go home. Eat food. Go to bed.
And start it all over again the next day. I memorized the
shelves. I could get there and back with my eyes closed.
I was determined and stressed. I found others like me
and yet did not have the courage to speak to them. It
seems souls are solitary beings, difficult to initiate conversation with, yet so brilliant and kind natured. Not a
single soul was overtly rude; very few even attempted
to speak to anyone other than their caretakers, if they
even had one with them. It hadn't occurred to me that
it would take this long; how could it? It's not like you
actually check books or files out of this library, right?

When Gabe would come in to check on me, many
knew who he was. I thought that was strange, but I figured, eh, he must get around—which I would never tell
him; I kept that little dirty thought to myself. It seemed
he could read my mind, though, so technically he may

have already known. But he never said a word on the matter, even if his keen smile increased in frequency as he talked to me. He would always come in and then disappear a few shelves down, more often than not saying hello and goodbye in the process, to the point I was growing accustomed to the pleasantries and even began to look forward to them. The days I felt the most discouraged he would walk me home and of course raid my fridge for a crisp apple.

"You need to be patient. You do not have a deadline, so relax; it will come when you are ready," he would tell me.

"Um, I think I have been more than patient. I have searched the shelves so often I can practically name every Garcia born between 1988 and 1960." This surprisingly gave Gabe a laugh, one of his infectious laughs, which you couldn't help but join in on.

"I promise you, Carol, you will find what you are looking for."

"Thanks. But can you at least tell me if I am doing something wrong? Looking in the wrong place? Anything to point me in the right direction?"

"You are doing exactly what you are meant to do. Just keep going. This is all I can tell you."

I needed to get my mind off things; I couldn't take everything being about me for this long. I tried a hand at prodding Gabe about his life; maybe hearing about someone else would help me regain a sense of reality or some sort of grounding.

"How was your journey, Gabe? Did your caretaker help you?"

"Carol, first, I know what you are doing; second, you and I know I never lived a human life. I was made a caretaker by him and have known nothing else."

"If that is all you have known, is this some sort of punishment—to work for all eternity? I would think that is a little harsh."

With a little laugh and a smile on his face, one that made his eyes light up, he said, "There is a way to get into the cycle; it takes many thousands of years, and you have to prove to him that you have done your service in its entirety."

"How do you prove yourself?

"You need to be the best caretaker you can be, to be able to steer souls in the right direction without interfering too much."

"So, based off your track record, can't you qualify to try your hand at a human life?"

"I have thought about it, and I know of others who have done so, but..." He trailed off into his own thoughts. How I desperately wished I could read him like he could read me.

"But..." I encouraged him to continue, gently of course.

"But there is more to it than just transitioning into a human cycle."

"Yeah, I'm going to need more than that."

Visually getting irritated, he said, "If you must know, when you go from being a caretaker to being in the human cycle, you do not retain your memories from when you were a caretaker. All the beautiful souls I have helped, all the knowledge I have gained, the lessons I have learned, this all vanishes. Think of it at someone hitting a reset button, it's as if *Gabe* never happened."

"Oh, I guess I could see that being a problem, but I must say, it doesn't sound like that big of a deal."

With a sorrowful face, he said, "It is when you have known someone for centuries and they no longer recognize you."

I could read the pain on his face, from the wrinkle in his brow to the glassiness in his eyes. For the first time since I had made my way here, I physically could feel his pain. Someone near and dear to him had taken this route, and he was devastated even to this day. I didn't need to read his mind to see that clear as crystal.

"I'm so sorry, Gabe; do you want to talk about it?"

"*No,*" he said decisively and abruptly.

"Ya know, Gabe, this isn't a one-way street; you can tell me things just as well as I can tell you."

"I'm sorry, Carol; this is just not something I feel comfortable talking about." His voice trailed off as he looked into the distance, facing away from me.

"Gabe," I said in my sweetest voice while rubbing his arm gently, "you know I don't care if you feel comfortable or not. You need to tell someone, so you might as well tell me. Get if off your chest, ya know?"

With a look of irritation and defiance on his face, he said, "No; moving on," as he trudged forward. I knew if I didn't get him to open up to me, two things would happen on that particular walk home. One, it would bug the crap out of me not knowing, and two, it was going to be a long, uncomfortable walk home. This is in addition to the major fact of him acting differently toward me from that point forward. So I did what I naturally felt comfortable with, which was to keep poking the bear.

"Gabe, what harm can it do if you tell me? I feel like if you told me, it would build a better bond and we could trust each other more."

"Carol, nice try, but I have no problem trusting you. Especially since I know your thoughts."

Pouting like a schoolgirl, I said, "That's not fair! Then you need to tell me. This is very one-sided, and I feel like you need to tell me so that I can get the most out of my journey. This is as much for me as it is for you, and if you are as good a caretaker as you say you are, maybe you should talk about it."

He stopped to consider what I was saying to him. It took him a few minutes to decide; all the while we walked in silence. I could see the house as we came over the clearing, and I knew I was running out of time, so I gave one final push. In my most sickly sweet voice, I said, "Please, Gabe, would you do it for me? I don't feel like I ask you much or demand much from you, do I?"

"Carol, this is highly inappropriate conversation between a caretaker and a fledgling soul like you. Why do you need to know? It will not change your outlook or help you in any way."

"It will most definitely help us understand each other more."

He considered it yet again as we approached the

porch where I had my morning coffee. "Very well, if you feel it advances your transition, I will tell you."

Almost leaping out of my skin, I sat on the bench on my porch, reached to the right for the ice-cold water waiting for me on the end table, handed Gabe his usual apple, and gave him a gentle head nod to proceed.

Disgruntled, and with a hesitating sigh, he began. "When I was made, there were few caretakers. It was always in the grand design to have some whose only purpose in being was to serve the souls that would transition through and go back down to Earth. This was a very smooth operation, but as more and more souls came to be, he needed to create more caretakers. The souls were outnumbering the caretakers and causing us all to become overwhelmed. The more caretakers he created, the more personalities were out there. This caused many caretakers to quickly tire of their positions and question why they were not allowed to transition as their souls were. Soon he decreed that certain individuals could request to transition as the souls were able to, but that was not something appropriate for all, since there was a catch—you would not be granted memories attained while a caretaker when you transitioned, unlike souls, who are given access to their memories of all their past lives. Now, all the politics never bothered me; it never pertained to me, so why would I care? I never paid any of the new caretakers any mind until one was assigned to me for training. Her name was Diana." He paused and took a deep sigh; I could see him wince when he said her name.

"Diana was taller than most and slender. She had bright, brown, almond-shaped eyes, olive skin, and wavy black hair down to her elbows. She always had a smile on her face; you could never make her angry, which works very well for our position in the cycle. She picked things up in a snap. I never needed to repeat myself; it made her training period much shorter than most. She had a natural gift with souls, a warmth you cannot teach—she knew how to calm them, make them feel at ease, and help them so they could transition flawlessly. It came as second nature to her. Soon, the student had become the teacher, as she would give me pointers on how to be more personable. As reluctant as I was, I had learned a few things from her; I had learned how to be more patient and kinder toward transitioning souls' needs. I had learned to have a sense of humor."

"Wait, you have a sense of humor? Why haven't I seen that! Why are you holding out on me?" I laughed.

"You have," he said with a straight face.

"Umm," I said lightheartedly, "no, nope, can't say that I have."

"Yes, you have," he said, irritated. "Moving on. Diana had this laugh, one that would bring a smile to any soul's face." As he said this a sweet smile crept across his own. "It quickly became time for her to be on her own. It wasn't long before I realized how much I missed her company. And it wasn't too long before she sought me out for the same reason; she had missed me as I had her. We spent any free time we had together. I would show her all the places to explore and things to see. I taught her the ins and outs of the library, and she taught me how to enjoy the life we were given. She didn't know, but just by being in it, she gave me the ability to enjoy this existence I once thought only a job."

"That is so sweet," I cooed.

"Yes; she was a sweet caretaker. Anyway, it had been centuries of us growing closer together—great friends. We created a sort of team; I would help her with her souls, and she would help with mine. Especially back in what you call the Dark Ages, we needed to help each other out. Souls then had excessive amounts of baggage; most thought themselves to be horrible sinners for the most mundane things. There were periods where humans were killed at such a high rate, we caretakers couldn't tell which ones were coming or going! It was a very trying time in history. In fact, you can still see some souls at the library from that time period; they are so set on the idea that they have done wrong they will not allow themselves to transition, no matter what. This also was the time where purgatory became necessary. Too many were riddled with guilt. Diana and I were seen together for so long that others saw us as a couple, but this was strictly forbidden."

"Forbidden? Why?"

"We were not built to be romantic with others, and it would conflict with our jobs. As it is on Earth, working with your other half makes things, to put it nicely, messy. He viewed us the same way in that regard."

"Ah, I see; makes sense."

"Now, to continue, Diana began to tire of her job

duties; especially after the Dark Ages, she would talk with her souls about Earth and before long had grown to be jealous of their abilities, as she was not allowed the same things in heaven. She saw those who had transitioned, and though all the knowledge in the world was at her fingertips, she begged for the ignorance that was human life on Earth. After all, cities were being built, science began to replace deities, art was flourishing. How could this not fascinate her? She would avoid asking me, but it was obvious what she wanted. She couldn't hide it from me if she tried. So she built up the courage to ask him, and that is when he told her the awful choice she would need to make..."

Seeing Gabe's sadness and frustration, I took his hand in my own and rubbed it gently. His skin was soft and smooth, perfectly manicured as well. For a moment I became distracted by his physical perfection; it almost made me jealous.

"He told her she could transition if her heart so desired, but the conditions were that she would never hold the memories of her past in heaven; she would start as a fresh soul transitioning for the first time. Not having her memories would free her of many of the things she had learned and begged to forget, but it would also free her of her memories of me and any she cherished. When she told me, I was in shock that I had even been mentioned. I knew he knew and saw everything, but we had never done anything or bent any rules, so why he had said something was baffling. She tried to convince him that there was nothing going on between us, but he just dismissed the whole conversation. He is the only one who not only knows your thoughts but can also predict your heart, so it was obvious he knew our hearts' desires before we did. He knew of her love for me and told her that unless I transitioned with her, we would never be able to be together again, asking her to take this into careful consideration."

"Wow. That…that is tough. So basically she had a few choices—wait around for you to go with her, stay here and just be friends, or move on and forget every memory of you?"

"Yes," Gabe said with a deep, depressed exhale. "She came running to me after he told her this and begged me to join her; I had never expressed my feelings for her to her, so she took a leap of faith in trying to convince me. Our bond had always gone unspoken, our connection built in silence over centuries."

"Well, what did you say?"

"I said no. I couldn't leave my souls on their own, and to be quite honest, I was scared. I had begun to receive more and more complex cases, and the pains of earthly life terrified me. Far too unpredictable, too devastating, and too emotional. I could not bear taking that risk without knowing the outcome. She tried time and time again to convince me to come with her. She did not want to go without me. Before long her smiles slowly faded, and her lighthearted nature went along with it. She grew tired quite frequently and spoke less and less each time I saw her. It pained me to see it, but I did not want to go. I did not want to transition; I was happy where I was. That is when I needed to make the tough decision to let her go."

With his head barely lifted from his chest and his voice faltering, he continued, "I convinced her to come with me one day to the library; I took her to the very top of the lighthouse and into the last room at the top of the stairs. I sat her down in front of the screen and showed her the Earth as she saw it. I showed her the happy families, the frolicking animals, the sweet babies, the beauty in nature, everything that filled her heart with joy, and I told her that it was time. She needed to think of herself first and let me go. I told her I could not be with her for this journey and that she needed to continue on her own. She needed to go back to him that day and have him begin her transition. She stood up from the chair and with tears streaming down her sun-kissed face, wrapped her arms around my neck and kissed me. My knees quivered, and I grabbed the chair so I would not fall to the ground. When I regained my strength, I ushered her to the door, and with one last, long hug, she disappeared from my arms. I let her go; she needed it…I needed it. I could not stand being the reason for her despair."

It was such a beautifully tragic story. All I could muster was "Wow."

"After letting her leave, I couldn't take it any longer; I needed to sit down so as to avoid collapsing with grief. With my head in my hands and millions of thoughts and images running through my head, I looked up to see the screen turn on for me. It showed me all the things I had feared for her on Earth, all the famine, destruction, disease, devastation, and sadness Earth held, confirming my deepest fears for her. Then at the end it showed me something that to this very moment I can describe in the minutest detail, down to the color of the room. It showed me Diana as a child; I could tell it was her from the brightness of her soul. She was smiling, laughing, and giggling. It brought tears to my eyes to just see her face. I knew then that she would be ok. My Diana was gone from me forever but free and happy to finally live."

With tears streaming down my face and the lasting images in my head, I tried to comfort him as best I could. I now knew why he had not wanted to tell me; this was a glimpse into the deepest, darkest reaches of his soul, and he preferred to keep people out of there. "Gabe, I…I don't even know what to say."

"Honestly, Carol, there is nothing you can say. I have spent over a century without Diana, and it has not gotten easier. Time does heal the minor wounds, but the deep cuts will always leave a scar."

He was so profoundly wise, it made it even more difficult to try and tell him something he didn't already know. Leaving the conversation for the comforts of silence for a few moments, in that time I realized that if he had been without her for at least one lifetime, that would mean…

"I know what you are thinking, Carol. I did see her when she transitioned back. I stood directly in front of her and even went so far as to reach out to hug her, but she did not know who I was. Even after she had transitioned further, I had hoped there would be some small part of her that remembered, but she didn't. She knew full well who I was but was denied access to my memories as well as her own. The pain I had when losing her increased sevenfold when I saw her and at that point meant nothing to her. This is what literally ripped my heart from my chest and made me dive so deeply into my own work…just to…just to…"

"To avoid your feelings?"

"To avoid everything. How could I ever love after that? I was unaware I was capable of such strong emotion until I lost her. Not only once, but twice! I could not bear the thought of seeking her out again after that; I do not have the strength," he said with his head down and shaking. He slowly lifted his head high enough to look me in the eyes; his bright blue, water-filled eyes pierced me like daggers. "She is due back in heaven soon. I would say in the next decade or so; she was gifted a long, healthy life from him, his gift for all her long and hard service."

"Oh no, Gabe. Will you be ok when that happens? You know I am always here for you, right?"

"Yes and yes. This time I will not make the same mistake and try to see her. I will stay away for her sake and my own. But mostly for my own."

"That is a good choice; you need to be happy."

"Yes. Thank you," he said before staring in silence off into the distance. We had watched the sun set in silence, and while the stars rose and the story replayed in my head, I began to wonder about the gift she was given.

"Gabe?"

"Yes?"

"When you said he gave her the gift of long life—was that a usual gift?"

"If you are asking whether he has given you a gift as he gave her one, yes and no. He gives each soul a particular, unique trait; it is up to them how they use it in their lifetimes. He does so for all new souls created, and that gift will last through all their lifetimes on Earth without diminishing or changing unless he deems it fit. I do have to say I have never seen him change a trait he has given; it is almost part of your DNA."

"Interesting, interesting. What types of traits are these?"

"Well, in Diana's case it was long life; in others it could be prosperous life, the ability to bear many children, ability to store knowledge, physical talents, musical talents, other artistic talents, things of that nature."

"I like that; so that is the connection we have with our past lives?"

"Yes. In time you will be able to know their lives as well as your own and be able to see the connection you all have shared."

"That's amazing; so what is mine?"

"I can't tell you."

"What!"

"That is all part of your journey, Carol. The trait may not be evident or obvious in your case, but you will see in time, or you may already know what it is. It is something that has set you apart from others. It is not always a significant trait, like I said; it depends on how you lived your life, on whether or not you utilized what you were given to its fullest potential."

"You know, sometimes it helps a person to answer a few questions instead of making them search all the time," I said snottily.

"I'm sorry, Carol; do you have something more pressing to get to? Are you on some sort of deadline? Some place to go? Some people to meet?"

Realizing fully what Gabe was getting at and that he was not serious, I responded, "Is this what Diana was referring to as humor?"

"Yes, I told you I had a sense of humor," he said, laughing at his own joke.

"Ha ha, Gabe. You are hysterical." I could tell he had tired of the conversation solely being about him and not anyone else. It was obviously making him uncomfortable to dwell on it, but I had one last question on the matter. "Gabe, after what you have been through, would you consider going with her into the human cycle?"

With a deep sigh, he said, "What would be the point? We would have no memory of one another."

"I see. I can tell you have thought of this already."

"Not a day goes by in which I do not think of this scenario—how we would live together and how life on Earth could be as great as she had hoped. But then I realize that the more realistic scenario would involve the Earth as doomed, as I see it. For that reason, I worry for Diana and do not wish to follow her into that cycle. Besides, if I went, I would also lose my memories of you," he said as he held my hand and a small, soothing smile came across his face.

Out of sudden shyness, I turned away to grab my drink as a distraction, and when I turned back, he was gone. "Now that is the Gabe I know." I chuckled to myself. I walked inside and headed straight to bed. But for the first time since I had arrived, I was unable to fall asleep instantly. I lay awake thinking of his last statement and then replaying all my encounters with him; his words stuck with me, and I just couldn't shake them off. That smile—was I missing something? Clearly, reading people was not my gift.

After replaying the countless encounters, I started to feel like a silly schoolgirl reading into something that was probably more in my head than realistic; I resolved to make myself fall asleep. I had another day ahead of trying my hand at the gamble they called the hall of records. Oh joy! I rolled over in one last resolute effort to go to sleep—and it worked.

CHAPTER 10

I woke for yet another day of library fun. "Another day, another dollar," I muttered to myself as I literally rolled out of bed, landing on my feet like a cat. I brushed my rat's nest of hair back; it landed perfectly on my shoulders as I stood eyeing myself in the bathroom mirror. I looked over my shoulder to the blank corner in the room, where something was missing. I couldn't quite put my finger on it, but something was definitely different. Giving up, I resumed my grooming. I brushed my teeth and took extra care in making sure my skin was clear and my eyes looked bright. As I searched the empty drawers for any makeup, only to come up empty-handed, I spun around and realized—the toilet! It was the toilet that was gone! "Ha! I knew something was different!" I laughed my way to the kitchen and grabbed my coffee to resume my routine on the porch.

That very same porch had been the setting of the distracting conversation with Gabe that I still couldn't get out of my head, but I knew I needed to push that aside and get back to the task at hand. I watched as the birds chirped and chased each other around the trees and through the fencing. They would tire themselves out then perch themselves up and sing their little melodies as if they were singing to wake the sun. It was cute; I always enjoyed their antics. As I watched them, I saw something crouching low in the grass. It was dark and moving so slowly and quietly that I could barely tell it was there; it only stood out in color. It was slowly making its way toward the fence and the birds when I jumped up to sound the alarm and alert the birds to flee. "Get out of here! Go! Shoo!" As the birds scattered and the animal came out of its crouch, I instantly recognized my cat. "*Kiki!*" I screamed at the top of my lungs, throwing the coffee mug and its contents into the air as I leaped off the porch and into the grass, bolting toward my beloved cat.

I rushed to her and snatched her little black tabby body off the cold ground and hugged her so tightly she squeaked. I smothered her with kisses, and—not going to lie—I wept a little. I was so happy to see her; I hadn't even realized how much I needed her until she was back in my arms. I had never been graced with a life with children on Earth, but I was able to have her and treated her as my own child. I spoiled her rotten, and she knew it. "How did you get here?" I managed between kisses.

"She got here the same way you did, Carol," Gabe said from the porch. "Because you made her part of your own soul in such a profound way, she was attached to it. When Kiki there departed from Earth, she naturally found her way to you."

"I am so happy to have her back! Now my home here truly feels like a home. I feel so bad she died so young, though; she wasn't much older than five when I was murdered. She must have died of heartbreak without me."

"Umm, Carol, I am not sure how to tell you this, but Kiki didn't die of heartbreak; she died of old age. She was eighteen human years old when she died. If my memory serves me right, that is a long life for a cat."

Setting her down on the ground and letting her frolic in the grass chasing butterflies and windblown leaves, I could tell she was back in the kitten-like state I loved so much. "Eighteen years? How could that be, Gabe? That means I have been gone for thirteen years? I have barely started my journey. How will I ever be able to find my killers now? My case down on Earth has probably long since been closed. Did they keep looking into it? Was it ever solved? What happened to the rest of my family?"

"Calm down, Carol," he said as he took my hand. This instantly sent shivers down my spine. A new sensation I had not felt before with him. "Your journey here is still on track. How life has progressed on Earth does not matter to you here. What you find here will not change how it will play out on Earth. Your goal is to gain knowledge and with that knowledge gain power to heal your own soul's wounds. Does that make any sense?"

Though my head was spinning with a million thoughts, I understood what he was trying to tell me. I knew where he was going. "So you will still be by my side in one hundred years if I still need you?"

With a chuckle, he responded, "Carol, I doubt you will need one hundred years to find out what you need to know, but if you do, yes, I will be here by your side every step of the way, guiding you."

This gave me the warm sense of calm I desperately needed after the realization I had been gone from Earth for so long. Since being on the other side, I had not experienced that twinge of anxiety you can feel in the back of your throat. Almost like you are about to throw up—your heart quickens, your stomach tightens, and you begin to sweat. I was grateful to be rid of that overwhelming sensation forever, until a moment ago when the feeling came back like indigestion after fast food! The revelation gave me new resolve to continue my search, but this time with a whole new method. With each file I pulled out, I was going to physically put my hand on and open up to find my man. I needed to know what happened that day and everything from that point on. This was my mission, set before me to understand my role in the grand scheme of life. Even though I had died prematurely, I was part of something larger; I knew it because I could feel it deep down. My death was not the end but rather only the beginning.

A few days passed before I could get back into a routine. I was so infatuated with my cat; as "crazy cat lady" as it sounds, I couldn't leave her by herself for even a day. When I brought her into the house for the first time, her food dish and litter were right where I had had them on Earth. The food and water in the kitchen, and the litter in the bathroom—she eats where I eat, and she potties where I potty. Simple, right? I loved watching her play. I could spend all day watching her. In fact, I did—because why the hell not! She curled up next to me as I slept and weaved in and out of my legs when we walked, slightly tripping me, but it was still worth it. We were back in a rhythm. I loved every minute of it. Even Gabe enjoyed her playful nature. He would pop in from time to time and give her a little hug and pet her. He would show up with some catnip and sprinkle some over her nose and watch her run around like a lunatic. It was an adorable sight. A sight I had to drag myself away from to get back on point. I needed to for my own internal nag to shut up.

The next morning, I proceeded with my usual routine. I crept out of bed, trying not to wake the cat, got dressed, drank my usual morning coffee on the porch, went back in to get mentally prepared for my trip to the hall of records again, and out the door I went. It wasn't long before I arrived at the lighthouse. The lighthouse was still breathtaking at any angle; as frustrating as this had been, the view made it just that tiny amount more tolerable. The amount of time it took me to walk there seemed much briefer than I remembered—must have been due to my resolve on trying to complete my task there. I began my search the way I had decided I would. Each time I took a name, I pulled out the file to make sure I didn't miss a single thing. Something had to be there. I was determined to find it.

Three days later…

I stood there dumbfounded, with complete and

utter disbelief. I had found what I had been searching for months, and it was a single file with one paper slipped into it. The paper read:

Ali Garcia
a.k.a.
Andre Menendez
a.k.a.
Alecko Rocha
born as:
Alex Alvarez

"I was looking for his alias this whole time!" I screamed, furiously shaking his file in my hand. I shook it as if it were his neck. I couldn't stand it. It was almost worse than not finding anything at all. Souls were shushing me as I ranted on about how this asshole had multiple names and it had taken so long to find out and that I needed to keep looking. "Nothing else! That is all I get? Just his other names! Not even a birth date? Not even known associates? Nothing!" I was seeing red. The souls around me grew more and more agitated with my choice of profane words, but I could not help but scream. The ground was rumbling, my rage was clouding my judgment, and as I was about to go through another fit of rage, Gabe appeared. He grabbed by arm, and in the blink of an eye, I was home again.

"Carol, look at me; you need to calm down. You need to calm your thoughts and your mind. Please sit down." He gently sat me on my own couch, and I just lost it, crying.

"I can't believe after all this time I didn't even have his name," I said through huffs and sobs. "I feel like such an idiot."

"But you aren't an idiot. The only information you had to go on was the name your father gave you. You did what you were supposed to, and you found the information you were meant to. The frustration you feel, you need to use it to further your journey. Use that to light the fire within you to finish your task. You will never be able to be at peace until you do so; this will eat away at you and not allow you to transition the way you need to."

He was making complete sense, but it ticked me off to hear it. I wanted comfort and not a lecture. I needed a hug for God's sake—was that so much to ask? But before I could convert any of my thoughts into actions, Gabe, with both arms open, took me in and hugged me deeply. At first, I was tense. I hadn't realized he would do that. I hadn't expected that from him; was it even allowed? I was able to relax enough to clear my rage and understand where he was coming from. "Part of me was so excited to find his file, and with the buildup of months of anxiety and the frustration, it turned into rage when I saw what little I had gotten as a reward. I couldn't handle it. My stomach had been in knots for one measly piece of paper that in a roundabout way was telling me to keep looking. I'm sorry, Gabe, but I just lost it."

"Believe me, this is understandable. It is not an easy journey to go through, but if it helps, you are only given what he knows you can handle."

With a few long, deep breaths, I was able to calm myself. Kiki had made her way into my lap and curled herself into a ball. Even she could tell I needed affection.

"Tomorrow is a new day, Carol. You can go back up there with your newfound information and find the answers you need. You are so close I can feel it. You are on the verge of a breakthrough; from here on out it will go by more quickly."

If nothing else, his words comforted me. I was happy to have the rest of the day to relax and be by myself. Gabe didn't need me to say anything more and made a graceful exit. I relaxed the best way I knew how—I buried my head in a book. I needed the escape into a different world to better understand my own. Before I knew it, I was ready for bed, to start the "fun" all over again. The mix of emotions made my head hurt. I was anxious to know more, angry and scared yet excited. I was on a mission but felt like I wasn't strong enough. My driving force was my anger toward Ali, or Andre, or whatever the hell his real name was. The more I thought about it, the harder my head pounded. I needed to sleep; I needed to regroup my thoughts to even see straight. I forced myself to slow my breathing and close my eyes. That's all it took to get my exhausted mind to get the rest it needed.

I did my usual morning routine and made my way out to the library. In no time I was nose deep in the *A* section of 1986. I had made good time and kept to my method of touching every file. This seemed to have worked last time; I thought I should keep doing what I had been doing and power through. It took me half the day to get through the 1980s, and I was at about 1978 before my eyes started to cross. It was a tough gig to keep looking at all the same names over and over again. Some of the files were so thick my arms were getting a workout. I also needed to look at them to make sure the huge file didn't eat one of the small files; this was probably how I had missed finding his file the first time! I wasn't going to make that mistake again.

Before long I had become exhausted and needed to call it quits. I wanted to carry on, but it just became too taxing on my mind and body. Here I didn't feel physical pain, but the fatigue did a number on me—my vision became blurry, names blended together, and I started to see his name when it wasn't even there. I headed home with my head hung low. Slumped into my chair, I didn't even want to look at a single book. My eyes couldn't bear looking at another word; I felt like I had been slapped in the face. I decided to roughhouse with Kiki and head to bed early; I knew what I was in for the next day, more tedious searching but hopefully less heartache. This journey felt more like a punishment on those days. What could I possibly learn from that? Patience? I'm already dead! Why make me wait?

I woke the next morning feeling refreshed. Though not unusual, this was not what I expected after the previous day. With the same protocol, I made my way down to the library and jumped right in. "No time like the present. I can't lollygag or I will be here for eternity—literally!" I amused myself. I searched for half the day, and then I found it! I had finally found it. In my hands I held the file I had been desperately searching for; I was shocked that I had finally found it. With tears in my eyes, holding his file with a death grip, I knew I needed to sit down before looking inside. I found a desk at the end of the next aisle over and placed the file down in front of me. It was a larger file; from what I could remember of Gabe's comments, that meant the person had done a lot in life—lots of events, whether good or bad. This actually made me nervous. Knowing what he had done to me, I understood I wasn't in for a fun-filled afternoon of happiness and joy. This file I could only imagine to be full of pain and misery. This file also looked to be well worn, unlike most of the others. The corner of the label tab had been dented down from use, and the file itself had dents and crinkles, clearly from being handled multiple times. "Or worse, by multiple people," I thought out loud to myself. "I hope this man was not the monster I can only assume he is." My heart rate quickened, my palms began to sweat, and my lip started to tremble. I needed to know but could not help but fear the monster inside.

I hated not knowing what had happened, but I feared the unknown almost as much. How was I supposed to just dive into this? I was scared just looking at the file! It was a lot to handle, to the extent that I couldn't bring myself to open his file, not just yet anyway. I sat there sweating from stress and anxiety. I felt the drips peeking out from under my hairline and running down my fore-head; the sweat dripped down my face and land in my lap. I just stared at the file, with souls wandering around me, as if time were standing still for me along. I knew I needed to make a move, but my mind ran through thousands of horrible scenarios, making the struggle that much more difficult and intense. How I longed to have Gabe by my side to hold my hand through this. I hadn't realized how much I needed him until I was face-to-face with my next step, which felt more like a tower to climb than a hurdle to jump over.

I felt a warm sensation on my hand, and this pulled me out of my trance. It was Gabe; he knew I needed him and knew exactly where to find me. He took my hand in his own and kneeled beside me. I didn't even lift my head to acknowledge him; he didn't even need me to.

"Carol, take your time. You do not need to worry; I am here with you. This moment will change everything for you, and I know it is a scary thought. Just take a few deep breaths. I will be by your side the whole way."

Just as he had told me to do, I took a few deep breaths and flipped open the folder. Without even real-izing it, I had closed my eyes before opening the file, and in that blink, I was transported to a room in the tower. I almost fell out of the new chair I was so startled by the seamless change in scenery. What tripped me up was that Gabe still had my hand while kneeling beside me but the file was gone, the table was gone and now in its place were a tissue box and a screen on the wall, which was beginning to show images. I wasn't sure what I was in for. Was it his life's story? Was it going to be like a scene out of a movie? I had no idea, and it terrified me into tremors—the tissue box didn't help! When the screen came to life, it brought back a familiar scene. It was the house he had taken the boy into. Ali was stepping out of the house and making his way to my car. He popped open the trunk remotely while constantly looking over his shoulders and all around him. It was dusk, and there just enough light to see what he was doing and where he was going when he reached into the trunk and heaved my body up and out. He glanced around one last time and walked as fast as he could to the backyard. He dropped my body to the ground—it landed with a sickening thud—pried opened the shed, and dragged me over the ledge into a cramped and confined space. He got out as quickly as he could, carelessly stepping on my hair in the process, and slammed the door behind him. He then proceeded to pull out a master lock from his pocket and locked the door shut. Contented after jiggling the lock, he walked back into the house from the back door with a slam.

This time I was able to follow him in, but instead of watching it on the screen, I was ostensibly his shadow and was physically there. He closed the door behind him as he walked directly into a surprisingly large kitchen; he locked the deadbolt, the door handle, and even the additional slide lock installed at the very top of the door. Ali took a few steps forward and, with a twitch of his head, seemingly was spooked by my presence and whipped around. I was staring at him—he was within inches of my face—glaring into his cold brown eyes. I wanted to swipe at him while I had the chance. Naturally

I tried. I tried to hit him over the head, and my arm went straight through him. Then I tried to scratch and punch and pinch him, but nothing seemed to work. I was furious, I screamed, and even that was inaudible. I mustered up every last ounce of rage I had left in my body, using up all the energy I could manage, to release the longest and loudest bloodcurdling shrill cry I have ever done in my entire existence. This is when I could hear Gabe in my head.

"Carol," I could hear him say to me, "this is where you observe; you cannot bring harm or change to anything that has happened in the past. You are only in this moment of time to learn, not to seek out vengeance."

"I had to try. I needed to know whether it would make a difference. It's hard to sit back and watch while I am being killed, you know? Besides, if this was in the past, why could he feel me?"

"I know, Carol. You are not the first to endure this, and unfortunately you will not be the last. Please try to watch what happens; this moves quickly and will show you only what pertains to you or should matter to you. Ali could feel the change in the air you brought when you appeared. This is an aspect of time difficult to explain. Though you are only visiting an instant of your past, it is real time to him. Your presence will always send a small amount of electricity into the air because you are only energy outside of your human form. This may be something I will have to explain to you later." As Gabe said this, it was as if someone had hit fast-forward while we stood motionless and timeless in the center. The clock spun round and round, and the two men were in the home, carrying on as if conducting everyday business. The little boy was stashed away in a bedroom down the narrow, dark hall. The windows were barred, and he was not allowed to leave the room unless accompanied by either Ali or Aaron (or at least the man *referred to* as Aaron). Aaron seemed to be the primary keeper of Mason, while Ali was gone most of the day, from what I could tell in this brief glimpse into their lives.

Once time looked to be back to normal speed, we were in the middle of a fight between Ali and Aaron. They both stood in the run-down kitchen, and based on flailing hands and screams, I understood that it was now time to dispose of my body.

"You do it! It's your fault we are in this mess anyway!"

"Mess? I made this mess? Who stole the piece of shit car in the first place? That was all you, Aaron! I did what I had to do to get what we needed and get the fuck out of there! You think I am proud of killing her? She is collateral damage."

"Damage that could have been avoided! Why did you have to hit her so hard? She damn near bled out in the trunk. I am surprised it didn't leak as we drove! And now you think we can get away with using her car out there! Are you insane? The buyers are going to freak once they find out what the kid has gone through! You know they hate damaged product!"

"Fuck the buyers! They will put him through worse than we already have. Besides, I did good with that car. It looks completely different; I switched out the plates, changed the color, and got rid of that stupid ass bumper sticker so we won't get caught."

Throwing his head back and laughing, he said, "Ha ha! You idiot! You think a fancy new paint job and a phony plate will get the cops off our scent? They have been crawling all over the place looking for her, and even the family of the stupid boy has managed to extend their search all the way out here! Now they are looking for both! Face it, Ali, we are *screwed*!"

"No, Aaron, you are. I know how to get out of this, so you are either with me or you are on your own."

"Yeah, right. If you leave me on my own, I might as well join the old hag in the shed." As he said that, I made a lunge for his body. I wanted to tear him apart from limb to limb, but Gabe pulled me back with ease.

"This is the plan, like I said; you are either with me or you are on your own, but the kid goes with *me*!"

Angrily Aaron conceded. "So what is the damn plan?"

With a smug look on his face, Ali continued, "The plan is tomorrow night we go into the shed, roll her body in a tarp, and drive her down to Lakewood."

"Lakewood? That's seven hours away! Back *toward* where you killed her!" he interjected.

"That's the whole point, moron; she needs to be buried as far away from here as we can get her—within one day, so we can leave the kid here on his own. That way, when we get back, we can cut and darken his hair and give him a change of clothes so he is not so easily recognizable."

"That doesn't sound too bad, except for two things."

"Oh yeah, what's that?" Ali said condescendingly.

"For one thing, the smell—she has been dead in that hot shed for a week. You don't think that's going to be a little ripe for a seven-hour car ride? Two, how do you expect to leave the kid here all on his own for a whole day without him getting out?"

"Well, your first point is valid. We buy and hang a ton of car fresheners and hope to God the smell doesn't go through the trunk. Plus, I looked up the weather, and we should be able to drive with the windows open the whole time; that should help with the smell. It's either the smell or jail; your choice my friend. Once we get to Lakewood, we can get to an empty campsite and find an unused path and ditch her. We have a couple of shovels; it shouldn't take us longer than an hour. The second point—well, follow me," he said as he led Aaron into the bathroom and opened the top cabinet, next to the mirror above the sink. He pulled out two bottles, one full of pink pills and one full of white. He grabbed them and gave a little shake. "Courtesy of our guest in the shed," he said as he tossed Aaron the bottle of white pills.

Trying to decipher the label, he said, "Ambien? What is this?"

"That would be her sleeping medication. Mix that with these, and you have a little boy out for as long as you need him to be," he said as he threw Aaron the pink pills.

"Benadryl? Seriously?"

"Hell yeah. He will get the best sleep of his life."

"What if we give him too much?"

"They're allergy and sleeping meds, not crack! It's not like he is going to OD on it; he will just be out for that much longer. Besides, what we will do is feed him a big meal, put some in his food and put some in his drink, make him go to the bathroom, and when we throw him in his room, scare the crap out of him so he knows never to attempt to come out."

"What if he has to go to the bathroom while we are gone?"

"Do what we did with some of the other brats—throw a bucket in there and call it a day. I got this all figured out, Aaron; just get a good night's sleep. Tomorrow I will go out and get the supplies we need, and we will have her out of our way in no time. Then we are off to Madison and on to the next buyer. I think the new guy wants a redhead, a true redhead. From what I am told, he will pay a premium as long as the boy is young. I don't know about you, but I can't wait to get the hell out of this state. Too many suspicious people; we need to get back into the cities where it is easier to hide.

"Yeah, but *this* buyer was very specific about what he wanted."

"You don't think I know that? He will be worth more this way too. It will save him from getting dinged up and his hair will grow back no problem. I never understood what the big deal was about hair color on these kids. Those fuckers have some weird fetishes."

Time stood still after that last statement reverberated

in the walls of the run-down home. I couldn't believe what I was hearing. This had become so much worse than I had ever imagined. My jaw had dropped, and though I knew he already knew all this, even Gabe seemed dumbfounded. *These monsters bought and sold these babies like cattle.* I staggered backward from the room spinning around me.

"This is a lot more than I ever imagined. I can't believe it. I knew this nightmare happened, but I never thought I would ever encounter that at home. The area was always considered safe. We were told it was safe. How can something like this happen?"

"Nasty people are everywhere, Carol. They hide in plain sight. You would have never known this was the case had it not included you."

"There were always so many kids that would go missing. I guess I always assumed that some monster killed them, and they were gone, but not gone like Mason. That poor boy, that poor, sweet, innocent little boy. He doesn't deserve this!"

"I know, Carol. This is why it took you so long to get this far; he knew you were not ready to see what really happened to you."

"At this point I know what happened to me. I am here. I am safe. I died in the back of my own car on that day. But Mason? Where is he? What happened to him?"

"Your paths are intertwined only until they leave your body behind. That is where I can no longer help you. If you want to continue to try to find him, I cannot assist you down that path. Though it is not forbidden, it is one you will need to take on your own."

Nodding my head, I responded, "I understand, but until that point, you can still help me, right? We aren't there yet, right?"

"Correct."

"Good." We paused in silence to get our bearings and collect our thoughts—I more so than Gabe. That is when I realized my dad had been wrong. He was assuming Madison was a girl—but it wasn't; it was a place. "Gabe, didn't they say they needed to take him to Madison?"

"Yes, I believe they did."

"Is that Madison street, road, village, town, county?"

"Carol," he said gently, "I already told you I cannot help you with this part of your transition. If you feel you must continue, you must do this on your own."

"God. Damn. It."

"What? Excuse me?"

"Sorry! I guess I got caught up in the moment." I apologized as I leaned my head back and said sorry to the air above me, as if this would appease the big guy so he wouldn't get mad.

Gabe shook his head, and time began to fast-forward again. This time it just took us forward to the next day.

CHAPTER 11

"Aaron!" Ali yelled from the front door. "A little help here!" he said as he banged around throwing bags from the store into the kitchen.

"I'm coming; I'm coming. You don't need to yell. These fucking walls are paper-thin as it is. You might knock one down!"

Both men were outside unloading the car, which gave me time to look in on Mason. He was locked in his room, jumping up and down trying to look out of the barred window. He was too short to see out of it on his own but knew something was happening, and it terrified him. You could see it on his face. He was little, even for his age, but cute. He had blond, shaggy hair and bright blue-green eyes that were almost hidden under his hair, which was matted. It made you wonder how long he had been with his captors or even how and when he was taken. He was a little on the chubby side but was thinner than he had been the first time I saw him. I believed that to be from malnourishment and fear. As he jumped up and down, he whimpered a little. It was hard to tell if it was out of fear or if it was due to an injury they had caused him.

From outside the window, Ali had caught a glimpse of Mason trying to peak and pointed it out to Aaron, who then angrily trudged his way into the house, slamming the door behind him. Mason, who saw this from the window, quickly darted into the closet and closed the door behind him in an attempt to hide. He squeezed himself behind a dusty and moldy old blanket and pulled up his knees to make himself into the smallest ball possible.

After slamming his body on the door and unlatching the bedroom locks, which had been added to the outside of this bedroom door, no doubt by them, Aaron stormed in. He took a few mad looks around to room before he started to rip up the bed and throw aside the curtains. Then with a grunt he marched over to the closet doors and ripped them open, nearly off the hinges. This scared the poor child so much he jumped. Aaron grabbed him and pulled him hard out of the closet, and Mason cried and pleaded with him as he was thrown halfway across the dirty carpet floor.

"Please don't hurt me! *Please!*" he cried. "I just wanted you to see me, no one else. I needed to go to the bathroom. I'm sorry! I am so sorry! Please don't hit me again!"

Hmm, this kid is clever. I couldn't help but notice.

With his anger subsiding, Aaron believed the boy; he grunted at him and dragged him by his arm into the bathroom and slammed the door behind him.

Completely relieved, Mason took this opportunity to try and find something, anything, to help him escape. He was young but smarter than expected. He quietly opened and closed the drawers, looking for small items that could be used on the locks or on the windows or even to dig himself out. Anything he thought would be useful he hid in his pockets. He didn't know when or if the opportunity would arise, but he had a small stash of items that he hoped might one day save him. They were stashed under the bed in a loose corner of the carpet he had been able to pull up; there he had hidden bobby pins, safety pins, hair ties, a shard of glass, and a few very small rocks he had been able to grab before he was thrown into the house for what felt like eternity.

"What a clever boy," I said to Gabe as we feverishly watched him on his mission to find something more to aid his escape.

Aaron was becoming impatient and began to bang on the door. Mason knew he was running out of time. So he flushed the toilet and used the noise to cover up his looking in the higher cabinets; he needed to rip the doors open to get into the time- and rot-sealed cabinets. When he opened the top one, he found a can of travel hair spray and not very much else; he took this and closed the door quietly. He stashed it into his little eight-year-old-kid pant pocket and turned on the sink. He was washing his hands when Aaron barged in.

"You are cut off from playing in the water. What takes you so long in here anyway?" he said as he yanked

Mason out of the bathroom without letting him dry his hands.

"It's hard for me to go when I know you are outside the door waiting for me."

"Whatever, kid; you will just have to get used to that." He snickered.

Mason had gotten good at hiding things. He always hid little toys from his parents and would stash them in his own closet. Now he desperately missed those days and wished he could go back home. He wanted nothing more than to be home, in his mom's arms. As much as he had said he hated the overbearing hugs, he wished she were there right now to save him. Though he was young, he knew this was not going to end well for him.

He could only take a few steps after being yanked out of the bathroom before he was tossed back into his bedroom, the deadbolt locked behind him. Though Aaron threw him around, literally, he wasn't as afraid of him as he was of Ali. Ali scared him to silence. Mason sat in his bedroom, and as we watched him empty his pocket into his treasure trove, we were transported to a place I had never seen.

We stood in a well-maintained home with a well-manicured lawn and neighboring houses that all looked identical. This was a well-to-do subdivision; the homes, from what we could see, looked like they were straight out of an architecture magazine. Running around us were three smaller children; they were giggling and chasing each other with foam swords. A little girl and two boys. They seemed very happy. A woman who appeared to be their mother was keeping a watchful eye from the kitchen when she shouted, "All right, you three, get upstairs and changed! We are going to the zoo today, remember? Kylie, if you plan on wearing a skirt, make sure you put tights on. Mason, I just washed your blue zip-up, and Nick, I laid your outfit on the bed."

"Ahh, Mom," replied little Nick, who looked as if he was four, "you know I can dress myself. I am a big boy, remember?"

"I know, Nick. But can you wear this one, for me?" the mother said, seeming to slyly know her son would do anything for her.

"Fine," he said with his little voice. "Just this once, ok?"

"Ok, my little man," she said, laughing.

Then we flashed forward briefly to them being loaded up in the great big SUV, then being unloaded at the zoo entrance, the sign at the entrance blurred past as the focus was on the busy children wildly running around the car out of excitement.

"Ok, kids, you know the drill—stay together and *always* within eyesight of me. What's the rule again?"

All three kids in unison said, "If you can't see us, we are in trouble."

"That's right! Now what do we want to see first?" she said as we followed the lively bunch through the entrance and into the zoo. They seemed like a very happy family, well cared for and close-knit. How could Mason have been taken from her watchful eyes?

It looked as if they were walking around at double

speed. It was a slower version of the fast-forward I had seen earlier, but this time I was able to make out who they were and what they were doing. I could tell the kids liked to play with each other and play hide-and-seek. This was when I spotted Ali. He was in the park and watching the kids. He kept his distance and made it appear as though he was there for the animals as well. He was very good at maintaining his distance. He was on his cell phone half the time and the other half talking to the man with him. Before long I realized the man with him was Aaron. They had both made themselves so inconspicuous that if I hadn't recognized them from their faces having been burned into my memory, I don't think I would have noticed them at all.

They shadowed the family more closely as the day went on. As the kids played hide-and-seek, they made their move. The family had worked their way closer to the entrance of the zoo, and when Mason went one last time to hide from his siblings, Ali grabbed him. Mason had run behind the restrooms, where he was virtually undetectable and out of earshot of his mother. Ali had grabbed him from behind, clasping his hands over Mason's mouth to muffle the screams. As Mason attempted to fight Ali off with kicking and scratching and tried to tear Ali's arm away from his mouth so that he could scream, I could see Aaron fill a handkerchief with a liquid. In one deft motion, Ali pulled his hand from Mason's mouth as Aaron covered it with the handkerchief. Within seconds Mason was out. Before coming out from behind the restrooms, Ali readjusted the way

Mason was held to look as if he was asleep on his shoulder and quickly carried him away, putting his hand over Mason's face as if to shield his face from the sun but in reality to shield his face from his family and the cameras.

Within minutes the two men had made their way into the parking lot, and they got into their car before being detected by another soul. I recognized the car as the one broken down on the side of the road that suckered me into helping them!

"Let's go; let's go. Quickly!" said Aaron as he dove behind the wheel of the car. Ali laid Mason down in the back seat and ran as fast as he could around to the passenger side. He jumped in, and they were gone.

"Calm yourself, Aaron. Worst thing you can do is get caught now. Drive the limit and we will be at the house in no time."

Mason's mom was enjoying the elephants while her children were exhausting themselves playing hide-and-seek in the zoo. Thinking to herself that this would tucker them out so she could finally get some work done around the house, she glanced over her shoulder to do a head count. She could easily spot Kylie and Nick and knew they were looking for Mason. She didn't want to spoil their game so waited until she heard them to move forward and start heading back to the car. It didn't take long before her instinct started to get the best of her. She called out for her kids to come back, and when she saw the look on Kylie's face, she knew something was wrong. She joined their search for Mason, and after about five minutes of playful searching, she began to get frantic. She started yelling more loudly so he could hear her even if he was far away and started to walk at a quicker pace. She forced Nick and Kylie to stay by her side, and after ten more minutes of panic, she alerted the closest zoo attendant. In a panicked frenzy, he radioed the other attendants that there was a "code three." As if in unison the heads of all zoo personnel stood bolt upright. "Blond hair, blue eyes, four feet tall, and answers to the name *Mason*." The zoo workers, in a robotic fashion, dropped what they were doing and began scanning the crowd in their general vicinities. One by one, over the radios, you could hear "Zone A all clear" static "Zone C all clear" static "Zone F all clear" until they had made their way through zone S. This took some time giving the mother ample opportunity to drag her kids in every direction in search of her son. She went so far as to jump up on benches, screaming his name, not caring one bit that it was scaring the other patrons. Once the last zone was cleared over the radio, an announcement over the PA system could be heard.

"Attention, zoo guests. Attention, zoo guests. Thank you for being with us today and for your generous support. We are currently experiencing some technical difficulties and will need to have all guests exit through the north exit. We are sorry for this inconvenience and hope you come back to join us again in the near future." This was followed by moans and groans of nearby adults and children alike.

The message began to replay when Mason's mom flipped out on the attendant. "Technical difficulties—and everyone needs to leave? What the hell do you think you are doing? How will this help find my son! *Mason! Mason!*" She screamed in full-on panic mode. "Where are you, baby? This isn't funny! Please come here! Please! *Mason!*" She continued to scream, though her voice was faltering and failing her. Out of fear she was holding onto Kylie and Nick with such force it was bruising their little wrists, and they tried with all their might to get their grief-stricken mother to release them from her clasp.

"Ma'am, please calm down. It is in our procedure. We all know what to do when we hear that announcement. It is code for us to corral all our guests to exit through our most heavily surveilled exit. This way we can close in on your son. We can only assume the worst in this situation since he has been gone for over an hour unattended. Now, if you and your children would follow me, we will go to the back office and see if we can spot your son. The other attendants on duty will be able to get a description of your son as they help guests toward the exit, and this will help narrow down our search."

This clearly calmed down Mason's hysterical mother as she obediently complied and followed him toward the offices. She knew something was wrong and couldn't help feeling it was too late, but he was able to give her a sliver of hope.

By the time Mason's mother had made it into the office to continue the search for her son, Ali and Aaron were already beyond county lines. They were well on their way toward the state border and knew they would be able to make it if they kept on course, that they would easily make it to their safe house before the kid woke up. This plan went to hell when they hit car trouble. Two hours into their drive, they started to hear the knocking noise from the engine. Time flashed forward again. They were stopped at a cheap roadside motel, and the engine was smoking. The two men were arguing, and this is what stirred Mason from his slumber. As they realized their sedative had worn off the child, they quickly gathered him up and rushed him into the motel room. They forced him into the bathroom and blocked the door from the outside so he could not escape. The less contact they had with the kid, the easier the hand over would be.

"Aaron, go and get that piece of shit car of yours fixed! We can't waste any more time; they will have an alert out for him soon enough. There is no way we will make it over the state border without getting caught then; it'll be even worse if he gets away from us before we can get him to the house and out to the buyer." He was thinking only of the reward at the end of their task and pushing out all the potential negative outcomes if they were not able to deliver. A silent shiver ran down his spine when he thought of what happened to his predecessors. They had used those guys as an example, and it worked. Even the mafia hits he was all too familiar with didn't hold a candle to the level of intense torture they inflicted on those who disappointed them. Or worse, those who got caught.

Without hesitation Aaron left the room and began digging around under the hood of his car, smoke billowing in his face while he smacked around with a wrench, tightening whatever he could find that seemed loose.

The next morning, they tried their hand at getting over the border yet again. They needed to get to the safe house to regroup and stage the drop. They didn't have any other option. With the kid passed out from having been up all night crying, and the breakfast orange juice he guzzled down his parched throat, having no idea it was drugged, they carefully picked him up and carried on. The car lasted them long enough to get past the border undetected. The police had set up a border patrol to try and find Mason. They were able to pass off Mason as their little brother, sleeping in the back seat on a long road trip. Luckily for Ali they were not looking too closely at 5:00 a.m.; this was the only reason they were able to get out undetected.

Time flashed forward, and we were now at the accident. It was all coming together now. The accident was not an accident at all. Their car had broken down yet again, and this time they were desperate, since Mason was awake. They tried to calm him down but were getting tired of the screaming, squirming kid who kept trying to escape. They saw their opportunity when they saw me driving down the road, minding my own business. I had innocently thought Mason was their little brother, a lie they had obviously gotten comfortable with. And when my back was turned, they took advantage of my generosity and gullibility.

Ali crept up behind me and with the handle of the carjack hit me in the back of my head. He then screamed for Aaron to help him with me into the back of my own car, and they did a seamless switch, no one the wiser. I was out in the trunk, most likely dead already, and they were on their way.

Mortified by the whole scene and completely terrified for Mason, I watched in grief-stricken horror as time flashed forward again. This time back to the house, back into Mason's room, or at least the room he had grown accustomed to calling his own. He was going through his items and plotting. He knew they would need to move him again, and he knew he was being sent to someone they called the buyer. What he didn't know was what the buyer had in store for him. But he didn't want any part of that, so he knew he had to try and escape when he was given a chance. His goal was to use what he could find and run when they tried to move him. This was happening soon; he could feel it. The guys were talking more often in hushed tones and were more easily irritated than usual.

From outside the room, Ali was pacing anxiously, waiting for the sun to go down. He replayed the plan over and over in his head and couldn't wait to be done with it. He hadn't seen my body since the day he dumped me in the shed and was becoming increasingly nervous and desperate to be rid of the extra stress. He didn't want the neighbors to see. He had had enough close calls in that house and knew they needed another safe house if this did not go as planned.

"Aaron, this is killing me, man. I need to get this hag out of our shed, and fast. The media is all over her disappearance and our car. It's not looking good for us if we still have her. They will figure it all out soon enough, and there is no way in hell I am going back to prison. Or even worse, they could send us back to Brazil. I won't last another day down there."

"You think the buyers care about us, man? You're crazy. You know that? They don't give a fuck about us; all they want is their cargo, and they want it there fast. We need to make this drop tomorrow. I already talked to Luis. They are going to meet us at that small airport just outside of the city. They have the papers for the kid and everything. We need to let his ass go and get paid."

"You don't think I already know that? They already have another one lined up for us. We play their game for as long as they want us to, or we end up where we started or even worse."

"I don't give a shit, man. All I know is that these sleeping pills won't be strong enough to knock them out for the length of time we need them to. I will need to hit up a club and get some of the good shit. You know what I'm talking about?"

"Are you talking about the shit you used on that red-headed bitch or the stupid surfer boy?"

"Both!" And they both laughed hysterically. Observing this was beginning to make me physically ill.

This is what they do for a living? This is how they make their money? I thought to myself. *This is disgusting!*

Gabe was next to me as I stood by and listened to their sickening plots and schemes. He took my hand and tried to sooth me, but it wasn't working. "Gabe," I said, "is this real? This is what I stumbled into? They... they..." I was so upset I couldn't even finish my sentence.

"They are human traffickers, yes." He confirmed it for me. I burst into tears. It was if my heart had shattered into a million pieces and they were sloshing around in my stomach, to the point I felt faint and began to dry heave. I toppled to the ground, but Gabe was able to break my fall and help my head delicately to the ground. I was nearly blind with rage and anger. How could people be so horrible? How could they destroy families and lives by taking these kids away from their loved ones?

The clock appeared to stop so that I could compose myself. It took a while before I could even be talked into sitting up, let alone resuming what was like a horrible movie I was being forced to watch. In fact, it basically was. This was the true-life version of what happens when all those kids disappear. So many families left broken and in shambles because they vanish without a trace. Poor little Mason had no idea what was in store for him the day he went to the zoo with his mom and siblings. He probably had no idea if they were even searching for him or that he was outside of state lines.

I sat up and took a few breaths, then stared directly into Gabe's eyes to calm myself enough to stand and resume watching this disaster. As I stood up and glared at the men frozen in time in their living room, I wished with all my might I could smack the hell out of them and call the police and do anything in my power to save the child. The story had changed from being about me to being about him. I wished desperately to know what had happened to him, and I believed that because our fates had now been intertwined by that horrible winter day, I was obliged to find out.

Once I composed myself enough to handle the scene in front of me, it resumed without hesitation. The men had ordered a ton of fast food and set aside a small drink and large hamburger with a heap of fries for Mason. They added the powdered pills to the drink, and for extra measure, put some in his food as well.

"Ali, don't give him so much to drink, man, so that he drinks the whole thing, pills and all."

"Good idea. And he won't need to get up and go to the bathroom either. Smart. That is the first thing you have said in a while that was actually good." Ali laughed while Aaron threw fries at him in response to the insult.

"Shut up, man; you know I was the one who pointed out the lady's pills in the first place, telling you we should use them for something."

"Get over yourself. I was the one to actually put them to use!"

Both men continued as they pouted over who was greater; clearly neither was a winner at this game. Aaron took the food to Mason's room and told him to call him to get the wrappers when he was finished (so they could be sure he had eaten all the food and drunk all the liquid). After not even ten minutes, Mason was finished and begging to go to the bathroom. This worked out perfectly for Aaron and Ali, so they didn't think anything of it.

In the bathroom, Mason quickly did his business and used the noise of the flushing toilet to conceal his raid of the cabinets. This time he found a container of baby powder and tried to stash that in his pocket but then realized it didn't fit. So he tucked it under his arm and prayed Aaron wouldn't find it.

He was hauled out of the bathroom and shoved back into his bedroom. It became clear the pills were working, and he had lain down on his bed and fallen asleep by the time the guys were done with their food. Relieved to see the plan was working, Ali checked on Mason and gave Aaron the thumbs up to lock the house down while he went into the shed to check on me. It was around dusk and had just started to get dark. This, too, played to the men's advantage. They did not need to sneak around because it was difficult to see.

Ali went to the car and backed it up into the shed—less distance to travel and during which to be exposed. He seemed hesitant to open the shed. He paced before it and would constantly look over his shoulder; it was almost as if he didn't know what to do. He had told Mason a lie about having killed Mason's mother, but in reality he had never killed a soul. He only would take them and move them from place to place, not kill them. I had been his first. This was the first time I could read true emotion on his face, true feelings of guilt, remorse, and fear. He did not want to get caught and for everything to unravel; he did not want to look at my body because that meant it was true—he had killed me. He knew he had enough on his conscience without adding murder. This was a new low for him; even he felt it. With a few deep breaths and shakes, he took out the key to the shed and unlocked it. After one final look over his shoulder—and amid my anxious anticipation and fear—he swung open the door.

CHAPTER 12

The door swung open, and Ali stumbled backward from the smell. It was obvious I had died and was decomposing on the wooden shed floor. The smell alone was enough to cause him to dry heave and to bring tears to his eyes. He had a hard time stumbling back to grab the shed doors, and when he could, he slammed them shut. With his full body weight against the shed doors, he managed to lift himself back to his feet but not without damaging doors. He had dented them in with force. Half walking and half stumbling back toward the house, he realized he would need help. More than just a hand. He was going to need a mask as well.

"Aaron! I'm going to need your help, man. Hurry up!"

"I'm coming; I'm coming! Hold your horses" he shouted at Ali from inside the house.

"Dude," Ali gasped as he came through the kitchen door, "we are going to need masks; it's bad."

"Man, you are just being a wimp. She can't be that bad."

"I'm serious, dude! It was so bad it knocked me on my ass, and I couldn't even see straight," he said exasperatedly.

Seeing that Ali was serious, he thought about what they could use. "Well, I think I saw something in the garage, so let's go look and we can get this shit over with." Both men then resolved to look through the garage. When they did so, it became more and more evident that this was not their home. It was clear this house had been left in haste by a family with small children. I had not noticed the small indications around the house, like the children's potty in the bathroom or the high chair in the kitchen, even though these were like slaps in the face.

While they rummaged through the piles of children's toys and clothes, as well as photos taken from the house and carelessly thrown in the garage, they found a cabinet of house supplies. It was half filled with rusty paint cans, rags, a plethora of cleaning supplies, and small hand tools. Like Neanderthals they ripped through the cabinet to find something they could use. Tucked behind a stash of rags and gloves, they found painters' masks.

"Ha! We got something," said Ali, showing off his find to Aaron. He threw him a mask and said, "Let's get a move on this; we are losing light." They ran back to the shed, and with masks in hand, they formulated a plan on the fly. "You grab the lady and drop her into the tarp I am going to lay out. I will then roll her in it while you pop the trunk. Should be quick. The faster we move, the easier it will be."

"Sounds good," he responded as they put on their masks and braced themselves for the stench to come. They heaved open to door together, and to their amazement my body did not look as bad as they had expected. But the smell was on point. It was obvious I had been dead for a while and needed a proper burial.

"Holy shit, man, this bitch is foul! Let's get this over with!"

"God! That smell is nasty! Do you think we will need to wear the masks in the car?"

"No, stupid; that would be way too obvious. We would get pulled over in an instant!" The men then did what they said they would. Aaron picked me up, more delicately than I had imagined he would, and Ali rolled me in the tarp. He heard a clink when Aaron picked me up to load me into the trunk but didn't look back to see what it was. They needed to move, and that was all he was concerned about. *Whatever it is, I will check it out later*, he thought to himself. The car was backed up and waiting to go. When I was sufficiently stuffed into the trunk again—which proved to be more difficult this time around with the addition of the tarp and the fact that my body was as stiff as a board—they struggled but did so in silence so as to not attract the attention of the neighbors. They both jumped in the car, ripped off their masks, threw them in the back seat, and were gone within a flash.

Standing back, fully stunned, I was shocked at their precision and accuracy. For not having done something like that before, they acted as if they were pros, minus the whining over the smell. I looked Gabe in the eyes and was shocked to find his eyes were welled with tears. The tears made them glisten and shine as if they were glass baby-doll eyes. Something so surreal I couldn't help but be shocked.

"It doesn't matter how many times I see the atrocities of human life on Earth; it still brings me to tears. I must stand by your side to encourage you to move forward, forgive, and forget, but my eternal demon is I could never do so myself, even as I must convince you to do so."

"Gabe," I said with broken spirits, "I don't know what to say. I feel like you are more upset than I am by this. I need to see this because I need to know. You have known what happened this whole time. I didn't realize you would be so affected by this." I then reached forward and pulled him into a hug. "I don't like seeing you hurt. It hurts me more than watching this has so far. Would you like me to tell you I can do this on my own and release you from this pain?"

He looked at me solemnly, with tears embedded in his eyes. "I would never leave your side, no matter how much it hurts me. I will never desert you."

For some reason, this statement shocked me. It wasn't that he cared so much; he basically had to. It was that he had said it in a way that made me feel like it was personal and based on more than just a caretaker relationship. This must have been just in my head, but I couldn't help but feel there was more behind his tears.

When we released each other from our embrace, the men had arrived at their destination. It was a campground/park area. The directory off in the distance said LAKEWOOD NATIONAL PARK. It looked gorgeous, a place I had never seen before but had heard of. The trails looked carved out of a J. R. R. Tolkien novel. The trees overhung most of the trails and narrow streets. The pine trees were all at least three stories tall; the maple and oak trees had grown so closely their trunks had twisted and turned so that they almost looked like they had morphed into one tree. They all had grown so tall they created a canopy under which other trees had been able to thrive. Moss had grown in place of grass, and it covered a lot of the ground. Small shrubs, vines, and flowers were sporadically placed throughout the densely gathered trees; it was so beautiful, as if they had been handpicked and placed in areas where they would flourish. Even the animals were placed perfectly—squirrels of all colors and birds swooping down from the trees to eat berries from the shrubs. You could still make out fresh tracks in the mud from the deer and could see little eyes peering out at you from behind rocks and fallen trees. This place had its own magic.

"This looks good. We don't want to go too far in and get lost, but it will be too easy to find the grave if we dig at the entrance," Ali said.

"This is your show; you killed her." Aaron snickered.

"Don't remind me, dude; let's just get this over with."

The men then struggled to get into a position at which they would be able to see what they were doing without drawing too much attention. They chose a spot twenty yards away from the nearest trail, far enough to be undisturbed but close enough they would be able to use the headlights of their car—or should I say my car—to dig the hole. They pulled out their shovels and within minutes were hard at work. The ground was certainly soft enough, and they knew enough to combine their piles into one to make it less obvious when they covered me up. If only they had used this ingenuity for good and not evil, they would have made great contributions to society.

Once positioned, they dove right in, wasting no time at all. They got into a groove—while one man was swinging back, the other was digging in. It took them what felt like only an hour to get the hole deep enough to not be uncovered.

"Should we go any deeper?" Aaron asked while measuring the depth with the handle of his shovel. It looked to be about the same depth as the handle was long.

"This should be deep enough. I just want it deep enough the coyotes won't smell her and dig her up."

"Good enough for me, man," Aaron said as he exhaustedly threw down the shovel and trudged toward the car. He fished around in the back seat for the face masks, and when he pulled me out of the car, he couldn't help but gag on the smell. "Oh my God, dude! She is nasty! How the hell are we going to get that smell out of the car! We will have to drive back with the windows down!"

"Quit your whining. It will be fine. Did you get my mask too?"

"Yeah I got it," he said as he threw a mask Ali's way. "Let's be done with this. I'm exhausted. When we get back, we will throw some bleach or moth balls in the trunk. That should cover up her stank."

Watching them, I could not help but feel my stomach turn. I was just garbage to them, something to dispose of; there was no attempt at a burial. They wanted nothing more than to be rid of the headache. I had never seen anything so evil and heartless in my life. To think, they only cared about me being found and eaten by the coyotes. That was so sweet—*not*! I hated this. I wanted to leap out of my reality and into theirs just to rip them apart, as they had done to me. It took every last effort within me not to break down. I needed to be strong, to prove it to myself, as well as Gabe, that I could handle the reality. It felt like each scoop of dirt was a tiny needle poking into my body. The first few were irritating, but the more they dug, the more it hurt. So when they finally stopped digging, I was relieved. Until they took my body from the trunk.

The men looked at each other with masks on and knew what they had to do. One on each end, they picked me up and carried me over to their dig site. They slowly dropped me in, careful not to undo the wrappings so that the coyotes would not catch my scent, and also so they did not have to see my face. This was a blessing in disguise, because I definitely did not have the courage to see my own face. It was hard enough knowing it was me underneath that tarp. I wished with all my might for it to be over, for them to quickly cover me and be done with the whole mess, but they did something that shocked me.

"Wait, I have to grab something from the car," Ali told Aaron before he could begin to cover the body with dirt. Aaron stood back and leaned on the shovel for a short time as he eagerly watched to see what Ali needed to remove from the car. It was too dark to tell until he came back with a small item in his hands. It was about the size of his palm but very distinct, once Aaron realized what it was. Ali had grabbed a small wooden crucifix from inside the safe house and proceeded to put it on top of the tarp. He then stood back with his head bowed and eyes closed for a moment. In this brief time, Aaron stared at him, perplexed; he had never seen Ali act in this way. In fact, he was watching with his jaw dropped from shock.

"What are you waiting for, slacker? Let's cover her up and go," Ali said to the stunned and leaning Aaron.

"Dude, really? Who are you right now?"

"Don't worry about that. It just...it just...it just needed to be done, is all."

With a shrug of his shoulder, Aaron said, "All right, whatever you say. I just didn't think this meant so much to you. You want me to leave you two alone for a minute?" He teased.

"Man, fuck off." Ali laughed and threw the first round of dirt over my body. They covered me up in half the time it had taken them to dig my final resting place.

They took care in making it look as natural as possible; they tried to place grass chunks around the site so that it would regrow and placed stones in places they thought would look natural yet would work to their advantage in holding me down in case of flooding.

Covered in dirt, sweat, and debris, they had finished their work. Satisfied that they had done what they could, they backed away and covered their tracks as much as possible.

"You think this is going to work?" Ali asked as they walked back to the car from the pathway. "I mean, do you think they will find her and know it was me?"

"Is that what you were worried about? There is no way they will be able to connect her to us. She didn't even know who we were. She just stopped to help us. It was in the middle of nowhere, no one was around, and we didn't even stay in the state. You will be fine; no one will find her and connect her to you."

"Yeah, you are probably right," Ali said, a little reassured. This had obviously been bothering him for some time, and the relief of burying my body had not done to him what he had expected. He had thought the weight of the world would be off his shoulders, but in reality, once they had walked away from the site, a different kind of stress emerged, one based on not knowing what would happen next. It brought worry into his mind, and this replaced the anxiety of needing to be rid of me. He clearly was remorseful for what he had done; he clearly was concerned for himself in multiple regards. He was concerned about the outcome if I was found and they could trace me back to him and was also clearly fearful of what that would do to his soul.

The men plopped into the car and slowly left the park, eager to leave but less eager to be caught doing it. Happy as a clam that they were out of the park, Aaron blasted music. Ali sat in the passenger seat with his head against the glass and stared blankly out the window. Next thing to do, in his mind, was to get rid of the boy—he hoped that would clear his conscience. He needed to make that happen fast. He had his mind set on Friday, but he needed it to happen tomorrow. That was his goal; he needed the out. He needed the peace of mind of having this job complete. It was the Murphy's law of his job—he was worried that the longer he waited, the worse it would get. He needed to get out of the area and move onto a new target and buyer. *Screw the East Coast; I need a new scene*, he thought.

The whole way home, I sat in the back seat of my own car, headed away from my own makeshift gravesite, and all the while thinking how horribly I wished I was alive at that moment to give them the justice I was now convinced they would never receive. I sat there and listened to them whine about how their arms hurt and how tired they were—the big babies. I was fuming. I was confused. I was mentally exhausted from the whole event. I didn't understand why I was still watching this; my leg of the journey was done. What more did he want me to see?

I needed the break, but yet we carried on. The car arrived at the house, and Aaron quietly popped his head in on Mason. Satisfied that the little boy was still knocked out by their concoction, he dragged himself into the bathroom, stripped naked, and took a much-needed shower. Ali, on the other hand, was quickly putting himself to good use. He was packing all his belongings in a suitcase and frantically making phone calls. He was making calls so quickly it was hard to understand him. All the words that I was able to catch were: "Drop, Mason, Madison, ship." From that I could only imagine what he was trying to do, and I was only there to watch. It was like watching a train wreck or a bridge collapsing, without any ability to help or change the course of events. I paced my way around the room and tried my hardest to move things, change things, disrupt his task.

I was so frustrated I took the closest object I could find, a lamp. It was small, composed of glass, and made to look as if it had real flowers on the inside. It had clearly been once thrown around since the flowers on the inside were mangled beyond repair. With all my concentration and frustration focused on the lamp, I threw it as hard as I could at Ali's head. It flew at him and made contact, but he did not utter a sound. I expected some sort of response, but it didn't even faze him. In fact, when I looked back, the lamp had never even left the table.

"I told you, Carol, you cannot alter the past. You are only here to learn. So please, be patient; we are almost through," Gabe said with his calming, reassuring voice. If only he knew how much it hurt right now, not only for me but also for everyone else these men had brought to harm. There must be a laundry list of victims; Ali had a file thicker than an encyclopedia, and it was definitely not for his philanthropy. Gabe's hand was in my own to guide me through, and I knew he wasn't lying when he said we were almost there. But it certainly felt as if he knew something was coming and he wasn't going to let my hand go. Ali was still running around when Aaron got out of the shower, but before I could listen to their conversation, time began to move faster. Their animated body language and facial expressions showed something was coming, something they did not agree about. Ali was throwing things at Aaron, like empty boxes and rolls of tape; it was clear Aaron did not agree with the plan.

Before long, it was daylight again. The men were asleep, but something drew us into Mason's room. He was wide awake and creeping around the room; he was gathering his things as well, what little he had managed to accumulate. He was obviously trying to avoid waking them. It was as if he knew something was about to change, but how could he have known? Mason put everything he had in his pockets and made sure his shoes were on extra tight. He had a plan in his head and was walking himself through it. His plan was to watch the front door for Aaron or Ali to leave, at which point he would beg to go to the bathroom. That was when he would make the escape. He was going to spray him in the face, stomp on his foot, and run for it. He was going to throw anything he could get his hands on at the other man to push past him. He knew this would be his final chance for freedom or escape. He knew it was now or never and was determined to find his way home.

Gabe and I watched as he prepared himself mentally and physically. He made little fists with his hands and threw punches at his pillow; he then propped up his pillow against the wall and tossed little figurines and the small toys they allowed him to play with to keep himself occupied. He had a bouncy ball that he wanted to use to his advantage. Mason knew how hard and heavy it was— if he hit them in just the right spot, it could topple them over long enough for him to make an exit. The trick was to hit them where he needed to. It was easier said than done. He tried time after time to hit the pillow in the center and would miss; he would nearly hit the wall, hit the floor, bounce it off the floor, and hit the corner of the pillow. He almost never hit the pillow dead in the middle. This surprisingly did not deter him; it encouraged him to try harder, but it frustrated him to the point where he threw the ball as hard as he could, missing the pillow and hitting the wall. It made a loud, resounding bang on impact. This scared him to his core; he was frozen stiff, too afraid to move, as if this would cause them to come running to hurt him. He stood completely still for what felt like five minutes before allowing himself to breathe or even move an inch. Once he realized they were not coming for him, he quickly returned to his efforts and learned from his mistakes. He threw the ball less harshly and was getting much better results. He hit the center of the pillow nearly every time. This excited him. It provoked a big smile and a confidence that he sorely needed. With contentment he stashed the ball in his pocket and lay in bed with his eyes closed. He wanted to concentrate on the sounds in the house, as well as rest for what he knew would be a great effort to escape. These guys were big, tough, scary men that could pick him up and throw him without batting an eye. This was the time for little Mason to focus. I wanted so badly for him to escape—after all, his wagon was hitched to mine.

Hours later the men began to stir. Their alarm had been a midmorning phone call from the buyer. Ali groggily and blindly grabbed in the direction of the incessant ringing noise to silence the horrible device. With anger and irritation, he answered. "Hello?"

A small, sweet, feminine voice on the other end said, "Well hello, sir; may I speak with Ali?"

"Yeah. What do you want?" he barked.

"Oh yes, hello. May we have the pleasure of the package delivery made to Pier Eighty-Seven off Baltic Street. Let's say, oh, three in the afternoon? Cash upon delivery, of course," the voice said with a slight giggle.

Realizing now whom he was speaking with, he responded, "Oh, yeah. Um, yeah. I am sorry; I didn't expect your call so soon." He had changed to a much sweeter tone of voice.

"Well, of course. No bother at all. Would the delivery location be sufficient for your needs? We are most excited and are eager with anticipation for this one. He will be a perfect match for our needs."

Though Ali typically was unfazed by the trades, this particular buyer was someone he had only been referred too. He had never met him, and from the voice on the phone was unsure if it was even a man or if he was speaking to someone that worked for him. From what he had been told, the buyer was picky but paid in unmarked bills, was generous with tips, and was always on time. This was all he needed to know in most cases, but this person gave him an eerie feeling he had not had before from other buyers. It made him visibly uneasy and uncomfortable.

"Umm, thanks. I will be there." He paused. "Oh wait, before I forget," he said, clearly rattled by the conversation, "what car should I look for?"

"Oh no, dearie, we will not be needing a car. We will be in the yacht, Pier Eighty-Seven. Don't be late; we have a date." Another giggle.

This was new for Ali—a yacht. With that kind of money involved, he needed to be on his best behavior. "Yes, I will be there." He tried his most professional voice. "Thank you for your time." This time he even tried to hide his accent. It was amusing to see. He was trying so hard to be something he was not. Someone white-collar, when he was clearly not even close. This setup excited him and made him nervous. He was curious about and terrified of the buyer. He wanted so badly to impress him, to keep his business, but had very real concerns regarding his own safety on this deal. He didn't even have to meet him to know something evil dwelled in this man, something terrifying and unnerving.

Ali shook it off, stood up, and booked it into Aaron's room. "Wake up, dude. We are set for three today. We need to get this done with, so get off your ass and make sure the kid is ready. I'm going to shower and look up how long it takes to get there."

Wiping the sleep out of his eyes and trying to compose himself, he responded, "Where are we going?"

"You will like this. We are going to Pier Eight-Seven; he will be in a yacht," Ali said in his most mockingly proper voice. "This buyer is a trip—creepy as hell, but a trip. We gotta look good for him, man, or kiss that bankroll goodbye."

"No joke. Give me a minute to get up, and we can figure out how to get the kid in the car."

Mason could hear their excitement through the door; he knew it was now or never. Today was his day. He could feel his luck changing. He had his own plans for whatever the guys had in store for him.

Ali rushed around getting clothes ready, getting the house cleaned up and wiped down of fingerprints, checking on the odds and ends of what was needed for the trip. He showered, shaved, and slathered himself in cologne so he could make the good impression he was hoping for. I could tell he wanted out. He not only needed the change in scenery but also wanted to retire. It looked as if I had haunted his dreams. Kidnapping was acceptable for him, selling a child to someone clearly evil was ok, but murder had him worried for his soul. Having murdered me, whether intentionally or not, was what was keeping him up at night. He could not get out of his head the image of a weeping woman. When this was over, he wanted to be done. A couple more jobs to get him set for the rest of his life, and he was off to retire in Mexico. Far away from anyone that knew him, and some place where he could blend in; most people see tan with dark hair as Latin or Middle Eastern anyway. This would make it easy for him to assimilate into whatever culture he wanted to retire in. He knew he would get more bang for his buck in Mexico. Setting his sights for the warm sun and cool drinks is what was driving him to wake up every morning.

As Ali scurried around, he grabbed the day-old newspaper sitting on the kitchen counter to write down the directions to Pier 87. When he flipped it over to find room to write, his face turned ashen. He was stiff as a board. With his hair standing on end, he was face-to-face with my photo. Completely shocked myself, I nearly fell over his shoulder to see what the paper had to say about me. In life, I knew I had not accomplished anything to warrant an article in the paper, even if it was the back page. The article read as follows:

Missing person Carol Anderson has been presumed dead after two months of searching. Her family had this to say about Carol: "She was a sweetheart and would never disappear like this in a million years. She is the most dependable person you will ever meet; she loved animals and was the best daughter, sister, aunt you would ever meet. For her to be gone this long without a single phone call or any information—we can only assume the worst." Carol went missing presumably Monday morning, disappearing without a trace. The police have issued the following statement: "We are saddened to say we do not have any leads on Carol's abductors. Her vehicle has not popped up on police traps or traffic surveillance in the area. She was last seen Monday morning leaving her place of residence as per usual. She then did not check in at work; this caused alarm within the company, which promptly contacted her next of kin. We have been searching ever since. We are at this time assuming she is the victim of a carjacking gone wrong. Her vehicle is missing, but her accounts have not been touched. We will update everyone if anything changes, but at this time we deem it fit to give the family closure." The family asks for donations to the Humane Society in her honor. The funeral will be held this Saturday. Please call Livingston Funeral Home for viewing and service details.

After reading the full article, Ali looked over his shoulder to make sure he was alone and ripped the back page off the paper; he quickly folded the article up and stuffed it into his wallet. He then proceeded to find another blank page to write down the directions to Pier 87. While he was busy looking up the best route on his computer, I spun around to relay my astonishment to Gabe.

"They looked for two months? They had been hiding out in that house for two months? No one had a clue what had happened to me after two months? I can't believe this took so long. Was there more about me in the news? Was it a large search party? Where did they even look?"

"If you really want to know the answers to those questions, you can check it out in the library later. I'm sure it is in your file."

"My file!"

A little bewildered, he said, "Yes, your file. Why are you so upset?"

"This whole time I was so consumed with trying to find that jackass's file, and I didn't even think to wander in and look at my own! What's in it? Is it big? Wait, wait, wait! Could I have just looked into my own file and found his name in there and easily pulled up his record without spending all that time searching shelf by shelf? Seriously?" I yelled, clearly upset at the idea.

"No, Carol. The file is on you; it isn't going to tell you more than just his name and how he affected your life. The information you needed to find you found it in the way you needed to find it, and you took the time you needed to take to find it."

"That's crap," I said as he calmed me down. "I thought heaven was supposed to be easy?"

"Well, it is." He laughed. "When you get to the easy part, that is."

"Not helping," I said as I turned back around to make sure I didn't miss anything I needed to know. I watched as he fumbled through getting the directions and writing them down. I could see Aaron popping in and out of the bathroom and once in a while checking in on Mason. He seemed content knowing the child was sitting in his room on his own and not causing any mischief, while Aaron tried to gussy up the best he could to make himself presentable.

Ali got up from what he was doing and proceeded to ready himself. He went into the bathroom to make himself proper for the meeting; he had already gotten his shower out of the way before forcing Aaron to give Mason a bath. This way he could get the boy cleaned up and out the door as soon as possible. He looked at the clock and yelled for Aaron. "Hey, man! Yo! You got to get some food." He walked toward Aaron and reached into his wallet to retrieve some cash. "Be quick about it too; it's already twelve-thirty, and we got to get the kid ready."

"Damn bro, I get ready then you tell me to bathe the little shit, knowing damn well I will have to shower again and get us food on the fly?"

Without any hesitation, Ali said, "Yeah, you got a problem with that?"

Aaron stood down from the fight. "Naw, sounds good. I am hungry anyway. Anything special you want or just burgers and fries?"

"That's fine. Just get moving. I will have this place ready by the time you get back. Hey, run the car through the wash before you come back too. I want it to look nice."

"Yeah, yeah, yeah. He is in it for the kid, not us, remember?" Aaron said sarcastically.

Clearly not in the mood, Ali snapped back, "Just fucking do it, and don't give me any lip!"

"Calm down, man! I was joking! Shit!" Aaron said and stormed out of the front door, slamming it behind him.

Ali was not even sure what had gotten into him as he shook off the encounter and the anger drained from his face. The mix of emotion from the shock of Carol's face to the eerie call and now the drop happening got him all worked up. He closed his eyes for a minute and took a couple of slow, relaxing, deep breaths before he got back into readying the house for their departure, wishing all the while to never need to see that miserable place again.

From a room over, Mason was listening to the whole thing. He knew it was happening, and his little heart had not stopped racing all morning. He didn't know when he would be able to strike but knew it was fast approaching. He pictured and dreamed of his escape in every way he knew how. Should he escape before they locked him in the bathroom for his bath? Should he wait and see if he could run from them when they tried to shove him in the car again, or were they planning on giving him something in his food? He was so hungry that I could hear his stomach grumble. Growing so used to the nagging empty feeling in the pit of his belly, he even came up with a name for his stomach: Oscar the Grouch. Having conversations with the grumbling made the nightmare slightly more bearable.

"Poor kid. I am in his corner, so willing to help, but I can't do anything about it! It kills me knowing he is stuck with them in that decrepit old house," I said as my lips trembled with anger. "Are you sure I can't just leap in there and pull him out? Or help him in any way, like unlock the door for him?"

"You know the drill already; I have told you a few times now. You are only here to observe. You are not here to interfere—you can't. This is already in the past, unalterable. You are here to learn."

"This is physically hurting me, you know that, right? This physically is making me sweaty and nauseated and lightheaded, and dizzy, and angry, and…"

"I get it, Carol. Thank you," he said sternly. "This is not ideal, but this is what truly happened. Unaltered, undistorted—this is the real story."

Becoming more depressed about the matter, I said, "I know. I just needed to take my mind away from it; I feel like it is going to break."

As I said this, Ali came out of the bathroom and ran into another bedroom. He quickly wiped down the doors and counters and flung remaining clothes into a bag. He didn't seem to have much—a few shirts, some beat up jeans, and a handful of pairs of underwear. The clothes he put on were clearly the best he owned. He then stopped in the mirror and fixed his mess of hair. He took care to comb it back with gel and straighten up his newly trimmed beard. He fussed with his collar, straightened his shirt, and then glanced at his watch. That set him off like a bat out of hell. He grabbed his bag and ran out of the room, going from room to room, throwing in odds and ends, clearly only his personal belongings, and wiping everything possibly touched down with a ratty, bleach-soaked rag. That was when I heard the front door unlatch. Aaron stumbled inside with the food he had bought from the closest fast-food restaurant. With drinks nearly spilling in his hands and a mouthful of fries, he mumbled to Ali, "A little help here?"

"Dude, why are you such a slob?" Ali retorted, visibly irritated, waving the rag in the air to show that he had been diligently cleaning.

"I can't help it. I'm hungry."

"You better clean yourself up after this. I can't have you all nasty and greasy with food stuck in your teeth when we meet the buyer. Grab some of those pills from the kitchen and smash them into the kid's drink. He needs to be out like a light before we go."

"I know, dude. This isn't my first time! Can you calm down? Here, eat a damn burger," he said as he reached into the bag and flung a burger at Ali.

"Watch the shirt! I don't have time to change."

"All right! All right! So sensitive!" Aaron grumbled as he went into the kitchen and grabbed the pills to smash into Mason's drink. "How many am I using, anyway?"

Hesitantly he responded, "How many did you use last time?"

"Three."

"Then do two. I want him awake when we get out to greet the buyer but out enough so he doesn't fight us on the way there."

"Sounds good," Aaron said through another mouthful of fries. With greasy fingers he smashed two pills on the counter and put them into the small fountain drink he had gotten Mason. After jamming another handful of french fries into his mouth, he reached into the bag, grabbed a burger and a handful of fries, and threw them onto a plate. He then grabbed the drink, swirled it around to try and dissolve the pills at the bottom, and headed down the hall. "Come and get it!" he screamed at the top of his lungs as he walked down the hall to Mason's room.

Famished, Mason sat at the edge of his bed and, once he was given the plate, greedily began to devour the fries. He knew to wait until after Aaron left to dive into the drink and the burger since that was how they had drugged him last time. He was definitely a smart kid who learned from his own mistakes. Aaron stood around only long enough to clear the wad of fries from his throat and tell Mason, "After you eat, we are going for a little road trip, kid. Be excited, you should have fun."

"Road trip?" Mason asked after pausing long enough to seem dumb, as if he hadn't heard them running around and panicking all day. He knew they were up to something. He wasn't sure what, but he was going to be prepared.

"It's a surprise, but you need to clean up nice so you can look good," Aaron said with a dark chuckle, as if he enjoyed torturing the young child. As I watched this, I couldn't help but make fists and ready myself for a fight. He left the room and latched the door behind him.

After waiting until Aaron's footsteps sounded far enough away, Mason opened his drink and swirled it around to see if he could spot anything, and sure enough, floating in his drink were small bits of something powdery. It was also lining the rim of the drink. He set the drink aside as he shook his little head with disgust. He proceeded to unwrap the burger and lift each layer to see if there was anything tucked away inside. Satisfied the burger was clean, he shoved it into his mouth so hard he got ketchup and mustard all over his face. He clearly had been starving and needed the nourishment. He wanted the drink so badly he was even tempted to drink it, ground-up pills and all. He tried to fight the urge, but the last piece of burger seemed to get stuck in his throat from his having inhaled the food so quickly, and he needed to drink something or risk choking. Panic-stricken, he took the smallest sips possible to spare himself whatever it was they had in store for him. If it was anything like last time, he would be knocked out for a while with no rhyme or reason.

After Mason had his scare with the burger, he slowly proceeded with the last crumbs left of the fries. He didn't want a repeat. "Slow down, stupid," he said to himself. "I can't believe I just did that; now I won't be able to be as strong as I need to be." He kicked himself verbally for the mistake. His face turned red from anger as he ate one french fry at a time. He wanted to be extra careful so as to not choke again and need to drink the contaminated drink. He truly was a smart kid—whether based on the unfortunate events that had befallen him after the zoo or a reflection of the way he had been all along. He had proven to be smarter and stronger than I had ever imagined a child his age could be. Never having kids of my own, or even getting close enough to try for that matter, it was astonishing to see the capabilities of this little human.

Once done with his food, he lay back and tried to relax; he knew what was up next, and that was his bath. "Do I go for it or do I wait?" he said out loud. "If I try before the bath, I will need to get past both and out of the house. If I try later, I may be too late, but I will at least be outside." That is when the biggest grin fell on his face. He had figured out a way—you could read it in his smile and his eyes. Even his body seemed to relax further into the bed. "Now I know. This will be perfect; this will be great! They expect me to be knocked out soon. I will give them knocked out, and when they least expect it, I will bust out of this hellhole...oops!" he said, looking around, then began to giggle. He didn't want to get in trouble for swearing but realized his mother wasn't around to wash his mouth out with soap for swearing.

Within minutes the door swung open hard. "Get up, brat! It's time for your bath," Aaron barked. Cowering like a small puppy, Mason slowly stood up from the opposite side of the bed and inched his way around toward the door. Fearing he would be struck, he tried to keep his back from being exposed. "Hurry up, you brat!" Aaron said, and he shoved him down the hall, hard enough to make the child stumble but not hard enough to make him fall. Hot on his heels, he followed the boy into the bathroom, watched as he turned on the shower, then immediately left, closing the door behind him, and bolted the top lock. He jiggled the door to make sure it was secure and screamed through the door, "Hurry the hell up too; we don't have time for you to play in the tub."

Mason was already hard at work and frantically searching for more items he could use to his advantage. He went through every cabinet and drawer to find something small he could use as a weapon. Knowing this could very well be his last day here, he needed to look twice as hard as he had ever done in the past. Satisfied that he had searched every nook and cranny, he resolved to get into the bath, thinking this could be his last bath for days if he was on the road on his own or, if he was lucky, it would just be his last bath in this dump, and he would be back in his warm bed and back with his mom. The last thought clearly brought tears to his eyes, which he angrily wiped away. Being that he was unable to drink the beverage they provided, he gulped down handfuls of the bathwater. It was obvious that the water filling the tub was rusty and spelled of rotten eggs, but this would be his only option, so he took advantage of it when he had the chance.

Meanwhile.

Aaron was getting his bag together and dressing himself in the least smelly clothes he owned—I could tell because everything he picked up he proceeded to sniff before he either threw it in a trash bag (which presumably he was using for a suitcase) or he threw it on the bed. Ali had already completed his packing and was busy pacing relentlessly throughout the house, neurotically wiping everything down with bleach. You could hear the shower running, and it quickened Ali's pacing. He was now on the verge of being frantic. After what felt like five minutes, Aaron finished packing and slammed his fists against the door to the bathroom to hurry Mason along. "Hurry up, you pest! We don't have all day!" It wasn't long after that the water stopped running, and that set Ali off like a jet. He went from pacing to pacing frantically to all-out sprinting from one end of the house to the other. He was hysterically grabbing items and throwing them into bags, then throwing the bags by the front door into a massive heap, all the while yelling at Aaron to take care of Mason and grabbing bags from him and throwing a new shirt at him for Mason to wear. "Make him wear this!" he yelled from across the house. He then grabbed the car keys and headed out the front door. Clearly nervous about time, he wanted the car loaded and ready to go. With the trunk popped open, he could see clear as day the dried blood from my head wound and could still smell the rot from my corpse. This stopped him in his tracks, and the smell hit him like a ton of bricks.

He paused for a minute and looked over his shoulder, back toward the house, as if he had just remembered something. He shook his head and proceeded to load the bags he had in his trunk. It took him two trips to get it all, and he finished by slamming the car trunk shut and pushing down to make sure it locked. He turned to walk toward the house but then veered to the right to go behind the house. He was headed toward the shed. "I better check to make sure it doesn't have anything that will follow us out of here." He walked right up to the door, and instead of pulling open the shed doors, he stopped in his tracks. He took the handles into his hands, and with the cold metal giving him flashbacks of what he had done, he felt as if someone were watching him, as if someone were right behind him, ready to pounce and catch him in the act. He knew there was nothing left in the shed to hide but felt like it was all a nightmare and that when he opened the door, something would come flying out or something would shove him in. With the cold metal handles still in his grasp, he shook off the bad memories, and with one swift jerk, pulled open the doors.

To his relief and amazement, he found nothing. It was old, dark, dank, now left with a pungent, stale smell of rotting decay, but otherwise completely vacant and void of life. He was expecting something more—perhaps a trapped ghost rushing him when he opened the door or a shed full of feds there to ambush him when he returned to the scene of the crime. He peeked around to make sure not a shred of evidence could be traced back to him, nothing that could hold his DNA or prints that needed to be wiped down. He walked into the shed and found a rag crumpled in the front left corner just as he had opened the door. He used it to wipe down all the surfaces, just in case. He was very methodical in his process, always going from top to bottom, and worked counterclockwise around the room.

Just before he made it back to the door to where he found the rag, he slid his foot left and heard a subtle metal clinking noise from beneath his shoes and felt the surface change, definitely stepping on something. As he realized this, he stopped in his tracks and looked down; he stepped back slowly and used the little light coming from outside to find the reflection on the item he had stumbled upon. Once he saw it, he recognized it instantly—it was my ring, the one I was wearing the day he killed me. He picked up the ring and held it in his hands. Completely engrossed with what he had found, he stopped cleaning, took two steps back, and was outside of the shed. He closed the doors behind him mindlessly and slowly walked away. He didn't make a single glance backward or have a single thought that did not revolve around the ring he had just found and how it was an omen of and cause for the emotional roller coaster he was currently feeling. He couldn't handle the feelings welling up inside him. Like a burning fire on his face, so strong it made his heart start pounding and his palms start sweating. He was beginning to feel lava inside the pit of his stomach rising into the back of his throat, causing him to be lightheaded and his vision to blur. It was almost killing him inside, but he did not know what it was—fear, hate, dread, regret. Once he named it, he knew—*regret* was what was causing his current state of utter distress. He was having a meltdown. The more he stood in his tracks in the middle of the yard, staring down at the small silver ring, too small for even his pinky finger, the deeper he went into the trance, as if the world around him might be crumbling, but he wasn't noticing a thing. The sharp breeze did not faze him, the noxious exhaust smell from passing cars and the noise from the surrounding busy streets were not even in the same world he was in right then and there. He could have stood there for a minute, an hour, a whole day, and would have been none the wiser.

Meanwhile, in the house, Aaron was trying to hurry Mason out of the bathroom and into his fresh clothes. His pace quickened, and he was so excited at the thought of getting the biggest payday of his life he was positively giddy. Shoving little, helpless Mason around the house in effort to urge him to go faster, he was missing the little details, like Mason stuffing small objects in his pockets. His pants pockets had become so swelled with things he was planning on using, it took a money-hungry, blind fool like Aaron to not see it. Aaron was humming to himself while readjusting his clothes then shoved Mason into the bedroom to give the meds time to kick in. He had never noticed that the drink was sitting there, tucked away, completely full. Utilizing his sleeve to not touch the handle, he closed and locked the door before proceeding to the bathroom to wipe it all down. Time, at this point, was flying by, all the pieces were in place, and it was their time to shine. It didn't take long to wipe down the bathroom; in fact, all he did was spray bleach bathroom cleaner all over everything then close the door. *Done*, he thought, pleased with his own work.

Once tossed into his room, Mason was in full escape mode. He stood sentinel, waiting behind the bedroom door, ready to pounce on his attackers. He had a travel hair spray in one hand and baby powder in the other.

He waited for the right opportunity to strike, and as he knew Ali was outside and they were about to leave, this was his last chance to make a getaway. He was so nervous that the little travel containers were slipping from his anxiously sweaty grasp. He stood in utter silence and as still as a statue—or as still as his little child self could be. Aaron waltzed into the room, fully not expecting what was about to happen next.

CHAPTER 13

A aron took two steps into the bedroom and blankly searched for Mason, expecting him to be knocked out and slobbering on his bed, and it confused and panicked him. When he did not find him there, he instantly stopped humming the little tune in his head and froze. His mind, snapping back to attention, took on a razor-sharp focus, and he stormed further into the room, ripping up the bed and anything that could possibly be hiding the child. All the while, he was completely unaware Mason was hiding behind the door. While he was shoving over a dresser in search of the boy, Mason jumped out from behind the door and jumped up on the half-toppled bed. Startled, Aaron twisted around, only to be met with a face full of hair spray and Mason shrieking in his ears. Deliriously confused and enraged, Aaron flew backward, screaming and clawing at his burning eyes. He stumbled for footing while desperately trying to rub the hair spray out of his eyes. It stung him relentlessly while burning like a hellfire, and the more he rubbed, the faster the spray cemented itself to his eyelids, ripping out lashes as if they were stuck together with superglue. Stumbling around the room, he crashed into the bedside lamp and slammed to the floor. This was when Mason took the opportunity to kick him and then made a mad dash for the door.

"Get back here, you little bastard!" Aaron screamed at the top of his longs as he uncoiled from the fetal position. He tried for footing once more, fueled by fear and rage. He was afraid of losing his paycheck, furious that he had been beaten by a small child, and—most of all—feared what Ali was going to do to him when he found out what had happened. He ripped open his eyes with his hands, fighting past the pain, and clumsily crashed down the hallway after Mason. "Mason! Mason! Get back here before I kill you!"

Mason was running for his life through the halls of the decrepit old house. He knocked everything he could over to block his path. He was managing to get closer and closer to the door, and his heart pounded with the thought of freedom. Aaron was closing in on him, easily able to leap over the hurdles the child was throwing in his way. Screaming obscenities to slow down Mason by scaring him and alerting Ali of the escape at the same time, he screamed out of exasperation, "Ali, grab him," as Mason was getting dangerously close to the door.

Outside the house Ali, still focused solely on the ring, was slowly becoming aware of the struggle between Aaron and Mason through the muffled commotion coming through the walls. It took everything inside of him to shift his thoughts long enough to stash the ring in his pocket before running at full force toward the house. He had just made it around the corner of the house when he saw the short, little figure of Mason darting out the front door. Sheer instinct and adrenaline had Ali hot on his heels as Aaron came huffing and puffing through the front door.

"Grab him!" Aaron screamed as he stumbled down the front steps.

Mason whipped around, with Ali on his heels, and threw the handful of baby powder in his face, but to his horror and panic found the baby powder had become a large clump in his hand and not at all of use; it had caked from the sweat pouring down him from anxiety. He then reached into his pockets for the rest of his arsenal and threw everything he could grab without slowing himself down. He threw a travel-size bottle of aspirin at Ali's head, followed by a few small stones, and finally a shard of glass. The glass cut his little hand as he struggled to remove it from his pocket, and yet it was what slowed Ali down the most. Though he was able to dodge the small items and was momentarily stunned by the aspirin, the glass shard landed directly into his footpath and sliced through his shoe like it was butter. He was down in an instant, giving Mason time enough to sprint forward.

My heart was pounding as I watched helplessly from the sidelines. I begged for his freedom in my head and, with a heart full of hope, met the momentary glance of

Gabe. The look on his face did nothing but fill my head with worry and doubt—where there once was hope. From the expression on his face and the knot in his forehead, I felt as if I could foresee the future.

With Mason halfway down the driveway and picking up speed, I tried desperately to will him forward and into freedom when, from behind me, like a bolt of lightning, Aaron came. He came running at full force, with a momentum I did not expect from him after he had stumbled out of the house. With two giant lunges, he leaped toward the unsuspecting and hopeful child. It was like watching a kung fu movie with a slow-motion, dramatic leap. He flew through the air with arms outstretched and tackled Mason to the ground, pinning the poor child's arms to his side as he fell with full force onto the cement, a grown man now on top of him. Without his arms to catch him as he fell, Mason took the brunt of the load with his head as it smashed into the concrete with a sickening thud.

Freaked out, I went running to his side, but the further I ran, the further away they got. I was unconsciously screaming for him, screaming his name, screaming profanities at Aaron, but it did me no good. They were still on the ground, and there was no movement from the child. I still tried and tried to rush forward, pushing my way through the unseen obstacles keeping me from reaching them. I saw Aaron finally pushing himself off Mason and pulling himself up from the ground. He stood over the child with his head cocked to the side and an expression of concern on his face. That is when Ali came rushing forward with arms flailing in the air and clasped hold of Aaron's arm to keep from falling to his knees. I could see this all happening, but it was drifting away. I was running toward them with Gabe standing by my side. He was unfazed by the race I was running, completely unaffected, as if he were floating while I was permanently glued to a stilled treadmill.

I gave up in sheer exhaustion. I did not want to give in, but I had given it my all. I could see the men, with the child lying facedown on the concrete, but as the images faded away, I could no longer hear what they are saying. I saw, through a slowly enclosing tunnel, Aaron scoop up Mason from the ground and walk back toward the house as Ali kept a lookout and stayed back to examine the spot at which Mason had fallen. He wanted to leave nothing of the event behind; he needed to cover his tracks. The images faded into blackness, and I was left standing in the library, face-to-face with Gabe. He had his usual, unavailing stoic look. He could read me, but I could not read him.

"Please tell me he is ok," I whispered through a parched mouth.

"I can't answer that, Carol; you know that."

"Please?" I said even more weakly. I could tell I couldn't hold on much longer.

"That is no longer your journey; you know what you must do to find out what has become of little Mason."

"But—"

"It is time for you to go home, Carol. You have had a tremendous day," he said as he reached for my arm, and within moments, with what felt like the blink of an eye, it all went dark.

CHAPTER 14

I rolled over in the flannel sheets, soft to the touch and warmed by my body heat. My cat curled by my side and purred at me with not a care in the world as I roused myself from my slumber. Kiki could always calm me. Whether by subtly purring or knowing exactly when I needed to cuddle with her, she was by my side. I sat up in bed; the simple task caused my head to spin. I could not get over what I had just witnessed. The images danced in my head, one after another. The emotions alone were enough to make me crash and burn. The fear I had for the child—I had grown to care for him as if he were a part of me, our fates intertwined. That is when it dawned on me—I died for him. I died for that child. Yes, I did so unwillingly and indirectly, but I still died for him. I stopped to help those monsters with that little boy and that decision ended my life. My good nature and large heart are what killed me. It was what had always been my best and worst problem in life. I always wanted to protect people and animals, especially animals. I knew of cruelty but definitely not like that. Every maternal instinct within me was writhing in pain and physically hurting me. Heaven wasn't supposed to hurt, so how could this be?

I could see all that had happened clear as day, like a movie playing in my head. I saw it over and over again, their faces burned into my memory. Not sure how long I sat there with my mind flooded with memories—it could have been all day, if not longer. Without human urges to eat, use the bathroom, or even move, I sat propped up, eyes wide open, and stared into space until I came to realize Gabe was sitting at the edge of my bed to greet me after I came out of my comatose reflection.

With a half-eaten apple in his hand, he said, "Good afternoon," before chomping another bite.

With eyes glazed over and a blank expression—not my usual leap out of my skin—I replied softly, "Hi."

Gabe gently rubbed my leg through the comforter and asked, "How do you feel today?" as he continued to chomp on his apple.

"I have been better. I can't get the images out of my head. It is something I will never forget. I feel insane sadness and regret for that child. Do you know what happened to him after he fell? He was so brave; I can't even imagine a kid ever needing to do that, and he was so strong through it all. What ended up happening?"

"As I have already said, I cannot tell you any more on the subject. Besides, you need to heal. You were not shown that so that you would worry more; you were shown it to close your own path, to begin your transition."

"How will I know when I am ready for the next step?"

"You will know when you are able to let the past go, when you understand you are not able to alter it and know not to dwell on earthly things that cannot help you and will only inflict more harm than good on others."

"Is it that easy? You make it seem so damn easy, like I should forgive, forget, and move on up," I said rudely.

"No, Carol. I am aware it is not that easy, but you asked for the next steps. That is what you must do. Take it as you see fit—your destination will always be there, whether you take a few days or a few centuries. I just urge you not to dwell too much on what you have seen. I have seen it firsthand many times—it will consume you. It will be like an insatiable lust, one you can never fully feed."

"I see" was all I could muster at the moment. Trying to collect my thoughts with his bright blue eyes staring deep into my own made it difficult. The only thing that snapped me out of the trance was his insistence on chomping down on that damn apple. "What's with you and those apples, anyway? Aren't they supposed to be some sort of 'forbidden fruit'?"

"Apple?" Gabe looked at the remnants left in his hand curiously. "Is that what this crispy, sweet, delicious fruit is? I had never had one until I was assigned to you. Is this from your homeland? Is this a common fruit or a delicacy? It is most intriguing."

I couldn't help myself; he was so sincere, and yet I burst out laughing. It was entirely too comical. I laughed so hard it brought tears to my eyes. Gabe, all the while, sat bewildered at my response to his childlike inquiries. "Gabe," I finally managed, "it is just an apple; you really have never seen one before?"

Still with that look of childlike innocence, having not lost a shred of composure amid my boisterous laughter, he said, "No. I really have never seen or tasted such a fruit. Is it something new? I believe there is a lot more offered on Earth now than what he originally created or designed. Is this one of those items?"

My jaw hung down as I marveled at the fact that something so common to me as an apple would be so foreign to him. It made me more curious than he was about the stupid apple. "It is common where I am from; they have at least a dozen varieties, and they come in multiple colors. Red, yellow, green. My favorite are the red apples; the green are too tart for my taste. Maybe you have seen a different variety? They are very common in the United States—that is the country I was from."

"United States? Never heard of it. Maybe that is why. I have not seen this in any other variety, my dear. Nor have I heard of your homeland."

"I thought you said you were on special cases; you really have never heard of the United States of America?"

"Oh, America. Yes, I have heard of the young country. I have had a couple of souls come across my path from variations of that name; none of them had apples, though. One, I must confess, had the most delicious concoction, however; I believe he called it a burger. Still makes my mouth water to this day as I think about it."

He always knew how to make me smile. "I forget how

old you are, Gabe, and how young a country I come from. He gave you a burger, you say? It didn't repulse you?"

"On the contrary, I found the meat smothered in the red and yellow liquid topped with thin strips of pork and then contained in seeded bread very appetizing. Oh! I forgot the fermented dairy melted atop the meat; it was not the same without that lovely addition! The combination of textures and layered flavors was highly satisfying. This soul always had them in his ice box as he called it. Most peculiar gentleman, died in quite a horrific way. He is a good example of how long this transition process can take, as he still wanders the library even at this very moment."

"What?" It took me a few minutes to decipher what he was even telling me. What the hell were the red and yellow liquids—then it hit me! "Wait, are you talking about the ketchup and mustard? And the pork—do you mean bacon?" I started to laugh as I pieced it all together. "So let me get this straight, he gave you a bacon cheeseburger with ketchup and mustard on a sesame-seed bun?"

"Why, yes, that does sound accurate. Is that how your people refer to such a wonderful invention?"

Biting my lips to contain my laughter, I said, "Yes, yes, Gabe. It was a bacon cheeseburger you were fed." He stood up and walked out of the room and came back moments later, with a glass of water he immediately handed to me and a plate with what looked very much like a wrapped fast-food burger on it. He sat down at the edge of my bed and unwrapped the paper, and his eyes lit up like a child on Christmas. Within the blink of an eye, he was nose-deep in the burger, groaning for air.

"Would you like me to leave you two alone for a few minutes? You are getting a little intense there. I don't know if you want to be watched."

He came up for air. "This will only be a minute. It is not quite the same as what he gave me but far superior in convenience with this wrapping." And he continued to scarf down the burger. It was as if he had not eaten for days—disgusting yet intriguing to see him devour the whole burger within minutes of unwrapping it.

"Are you satisfied yet?"

"Why yes, thank you for asking. Now for the reason why I am here: I am here to see how you are doing and find out if there is anything I can do to further your journey."

"I told you what you can do; you can help me find Mason."

"We have been down this road already, Carol. If you must know about him, you need to find that for yourself; it is no longer part of your path. It will not help your transition."

"I know, but I need to know what is happening with him. It is all I can think about."

"I know. I am here for you for whatever else you may need. I will continue to check in on you; you are past the hardest part and just need to find your inner peace." He stood up and started walking out of my bedroom when he suddenly stopped in the hallway and turned back to me to say, "You may find it beneficial to visit your father." Then, without a word, he swung around and slowly vanished as he walked away.

"My dad?" I said out loud, as if I were speaking to someone. I couldn't help but wonder why he had brought him up. Why my dad? Yes, he was helpful with what he knew before, but why would he know more and not tell me? Has something changed? Has someone else died, and they are with him? Curiosity got the best of me. I was out of bed and ready to go in only a couple of minutes. Kiki seemed content curled up in a little ball on the bed with or without me, so I had no concerns there.

With his words still rolling around in my head, I started for the door. Now that I knew the route to take, it wouldn't be long before I arrived at his home, but the path did seem extra inviting this time; this felt like much less like a chore and much more like a relaxing leisurely stroll in the woods. I was in such a hurry to find answers I lost track of the fact that I didn't truly have a schedule. I needed to know, but it was all just for me and my curiosity. I didn't need to report to anyone; this information was not work. This information was not vital to my existence. In fact, if they deemed it necessary for me to know, he would have shown me. I truly did not need to know.

I thought of all this as I strolled through the woods, through the fallen leaves, following the bends of the winding path. It was beautiful to see, as if by my will it was autumn in the woods and the colors of trees were the way they were only for my amusement and joy, with the thick canopy of luscious foliage of every color variety that autumn brings, bright yellows and deep crimson-reds. The sun-kissed leaves were the first to turn, while the more shaded branches were able to stubbornly hold onto their green leaves for what might only have been a few more days. The breeze brought in the crisp, sharp air that I had grown to love from my childhood; it brought back fond memories of playing in the huge heaps of fallen leaves. I slowed down to a snail's pace, forgetting the whole reason why I was going to my father's and enjoying what I could only now take the time to truly enjoy.

In life everything seemed so important—there was always a place to be, a thing to do—but now, though I had my sights set on something, it all fell to the side. I could hear the leaves crunching under my footsteps and the rustling of the wind—I couldn't believe it; I could actually hear the wind. It was very melodic, sweet sounding and coming through in waves, as if it were a song carried by one tree to another, something so simple yet so magical. "I can't believe I missed this my whole life and I needed to be dead before I could silence all the noise long enough to hear this and see this."

It was most certainly disheartening to know I had missed this opportunity my whole life, but at the same time, I was grateful to have the ability to enjoy it now.

I had made my way to the clearing where the woods met the lake. I could spot his little house with the chimney smoke. He sat out on the front rocker waiting for me to arrive, seemingly knowing I was coming. Seeing him again brought a smile to my face, one that did not fade until after I left.

I picked up my pace as I headed down to his house, with the sun glistening off the lake and the breeze singing through my hair. I made my way to his open arms. He always knew how to make a person feel warm, comfortable, and loved, something I had never been able to find after he had died and was so grateful to find again, waiting for me on this side.

"How are you, baby girl?"

With a deep inhale and long sigh, I replied, "I am good. I didn't think knowing would be so bad. They were monsters, Daddy. I didn't expect to be part of something so horrible."

"I know, honey. I know. Come inside. We will have some coffee and talk." With his arm still wrapped around my shoulders, he led me into the warm, cozy nest he had made for himself.

"Dad?" I asked as I parked myself on his couch.

"Yes?" he said over his shoulder as he struggled to carry two piping hot coffees without spilling them. He overly gently set his next to his recliner and focused all his attention on handing me mine through an extended reach, as if afraid if he came one step closer, it would be the step that would make him spill. I graciously stood and took the coffee from him to relieve him of the pressure.

"I love you, but why have you not transitioned yet? Why did you stay here? Gabe seems to think I am ready to move on, or at least is trying to pressure me to do so…but you, you have been here this whole time. Why?"

With a small smile, he said, "You know why. I know you know why." He sighed as he sipped his coffee. "I am waiting for your mother and your sister. I understand if you need to follow Gabe, but I was hoping I would have our family together again, even if for only a moment. This is what I have been waiting for."

Deep down I knew—even before he said it. But following Gabe? What was that about? Did he know something I didn't? I had to ask; this was definitely not something I expected to hear. I had come for one reason, and now there were two. "Dad, what do you mean you understand if I need to follow Gabe? Are you asking if I just need to move on, or do you mean something else? I am confused." I laughed at the idea.

With a little sparkle in his eyes, he said, "I see the way you look at him. I don't think you even realize it, but you remember the old saying, 'your eyes are the window to your soul'? I can read you like an open book, kid," he mused.

My cheeks burst into flames (not literally, of course); the idea had me blushing as if I were a schoolgirl. "Gabe?" I half asked, directing the question more at myself than at my father. I had not really even thought about it. I had been so involved in my own mission I had not even let myself acknowledge anything more. I hadn't even seen it.

"Yes, Gabe. Just because he is a caretaker does not mean he does not have the same feelings and thoughts that the rest of us have. Have you never thought about him? He seems very attentive to your needs. I have barely even seen my caretaker. In fact, I can't even remember her name," he said with a loud, boisterous laugh.

"I always thought he was attentive because of my specific case."

"Honey, don't be so naïve. There are millions of souls that are, or were, in the negative death position you have been in. I do not honestly believe they are being taken care of the way he is taking care of you."

I had to think about this for some time, but it still didn't make sense. Why would he want me? I was nothing special. I didn't have any great defining characters, nor would I consider myself beautiful, at least in a classical sense. Why would he give me extra attention? "Why me?"

"Why you?" he seemed offended by the question. "Why you?" he repeated. "Carol, are you crazy? Why not you? You are smart, and generous, and the warmest-hearted soul I have ever had the joy of knowing, and I am not just saying that because you are my kid! You have something special about you that I am sorry people on Earth did not give themselves the opportunity to see. You are something truly special, truly someone to behold. I hate that you are so down on yourself, even on this side. You should be able to look in the mirror and see your true beauty. See the real you. See the wonderful being that has brought joy and happiness to everyone who has been lucky enough to surround you."

I couldn't stop blushing. Yes, I knew as my father he

was supposed to say that kind of thing to make me feel better, but this was said so strongly and forcefully you could tell he meant it. Knowing that anyone thought so highly of me gave me goose bumps and sent a small wave of chills down my spine. "I..." I stammered. "I don't know what to say. I just assumed he was attentive because of my case. This has all gotten so confusing."

"Carol, this isn't about him. Yes, he is drawn to you, but this is about you not seeing your own true potential and denying yourself happiness." As he said this, he grabbed me by my shoulders and led me to the hallway mirror. He planted me directly in front of it, only inches from the cold, glass surface. "Look at yourself. Truly look at yourself. I need you to see what Gabe and I see."

Obediently, I did as he said. I looked at my reflection in the mirror to search for what they had clearly found. It was a little difficult, being that none of the features he described were physical. As if sensing this, he continued.

"Do you see that scar on your chin? It's faded away over the years, but you can still see that small hint remaining. That was from when you were a kid, do you remember?"

"Of course I do. It was from when Sarah pushed me off the tire swing," I said with a sly grin.

"Don't be a smartass. You know it was from the neighbor's dog. Now remind me how it happened?"

"Fine," I sighed. "The stupid dog—oh, I can't remember its name, so let's just call it Dummy—was chasing Sarah and got too excited and started to bite her. I pulled it off her as it was tearing at her shirt. I think her crying made it more excited, and it started to get more aggressive. I pulled her away from the dog, but then Dummy jumped on my back, smashing me facedown in the dirt, where my chin was busted open by a rock. The blood must have freaked out the dog, because he ran off afterward."

"Exactly."

"Exactly what?"

"You still don't see it, Carol? Instead of screaming your head off or sitting back and laughing at your sister getting mauled by a dog, you jumped in and saved her. You even got hurt in the process. That little scar is your daily reminder of how amazing you really are. You are so selfless, and you only had concern for her safety and not your own."

"I think you are being a little overly generous. It wasn't that bad."

"Fine. If you don't believe me, look at your shirt."

"My shirt?" This one definitely confused me.

"Yes, that cheap sweater you are wearing."

"That's a little harsh!" I blurted out at the offensive comment.

"Carol! You made a substantial amount of money in your job, and what did you spend all your money on? What did you waste all your time on? What did you decide was a better way of spending a Saturday night than going out with the other young ladies to find a man? What was it you always used to tell me?"

Blushing a little at what he was trying to get me to

confess to, I replied, "I would say I would rather stay home and take care of the rescue animals and run the books for the charity..." I trailed off. I was starting to see his point. I had never done anything horrible in my life—well, maybe besides cheat on a calculus test in high school; other than that, I was a good girl. I always did as I was told, and even when it came to relationships, I was very conservative. I lost interest in being the girl who needed a husband and was more interested in saving things that could not help themselves. He was referring to my inner beauty, the thing that set me apart from all the "pretty girls" I was faced with in life.

"I think you are finally starting to see what I always knew to be true. You spent all your time and money helping others. You are selfless; you would rather give away all your belongings and live off the land so as not to convenience anyone else, and you never cared about making yourself stand out in a crowd. Never once did you talk back or even rebel—and trust me, we expected a full-blown rebellion from you, but it never came. You were such a good person that you almost disappeared before you even died. You were the angel for many people, many who did not even get the chance to know your name. You even died trying to be selfless."

Tears began streaming down my face. It took him holding me in front of a mirror after death to find my self-worth. Whether it was me finally finding myself or it was the fact that I had missed my opportunity in life to do so that made me cry, I was unsure, but tears raced down my cheeks either way. I wiped them away quickly, and with every swipe of my hand and bat of my lash, I could see myself more clearly in the mirror. With every wiped-away tear, I was becoming physically more beautiful. The wrinkles under my eyes and around my lips were fading; the color in my cheeks and lips was becoming rosier. My eyes—even my eyes became brighter and more vibrant. It was as if I was changing from Technicolor to high-definition! My smile grew straighter and my teeth whiter. My hair even seemed to flip itself into a much richer tone, something more caramel and warmer than I had ever been able to achieve from a box in life. Fearing it was a mind trick, I covered my face with my hands and shook myself to knock myself out of any trick I had played on myself.

Through cracked fingers I slowly looked in the mirror. I was astonished by what was facing back at me; it was my own face, but with every natural sign of beauty amplified in a way I never could have imagined. I shrieked with joy, jolting my father out of his gaze.

"Carol, this is the real you! This is what I would see when I looked at you. I did not see that other woman, the one you let yourself become to cover your insecurities. Do you see this?" He grabbed my hands and spun me around, dancing. "Do you see yourself now? You are finally letting your light shine through! You are so beautiful! This has been a long time coming!"

My face crimson from trying to wipe away my tears, I was overjoyed with the change. I had no idea finding myself would cause such a drastic change in my appearance. I stood parked in front of the mirror, thinking if

I dared to move away, look away, or even take too long of a blink, I would turn back into the nothingness I had been before.

Satisfied I would not wither away, I pulled myself from the mirror and sat back down on the couch. With a grin on my face and coffee in my hand, I felt like a whole new woman, someone much more content with herself, someone much more confident in her personality and in her own skin.

"Now that I have my Carol, I am all ears. You came to me for a reason—clearly getting more than you bargained for, aren't you?"

I laughed. "Yes, well, I guess that depends on what other information you have for me."

From his heavy sigh, I could tell he knew something I certainly did not know. "Carol, you have to remember this is not your journey. I only know because after you died I was given information; Gabe knew you would come to me. I did not want to know."

"Are you talking about Mason? My main concern is for the boy; my other question is whether anyone ever found my body."

"I can't help you with everything, but I do know they have not found your body, and for a very long time they won't. From what I have been told, when your body is found, it is too far gone to DNA test; they are able to find you only by your dental records."

I gasped and had a gut-wrenching feeling in the pit of my stomach. He continued, "From what I have seen, your body was found by hikers who had lost their dog.

The dog ventured off the path and must have found your scent. The hikers found him..." He stopped and with a grave face, shuddered.

"Dad, I need to know. I don't think I will have closure until you tell me."

"Honey, I hate knowing. I can't even imagine how you will feel knowing he was gnawing on your arm bone when they found him. Oh no. I...I...I am so sorry; I didn't mean to break it to you like this!"

After the room stopped spinning, I took a sip from my coffee mug, which I was unintentionally white-knuckling. I looked into my father's concerned eyes and realized a few things at that moment. One, it was only a body, nothing more than a carcass that I had hoped would be buried in a more civilized manner so that it would not become a hound's chew toy. Two, my father, even after death, would never cease to amaze me with how devoted he was to his wife and children. "Dad." I finally spoke. "I'm ok. I just needed to know. After they found me being the dog's chew toy, what happened?"

Relieved at how calm I was, he said, "Well, after the hikers removed you from their dog's mouth, they called the police, who then exhumed the body and, based on your dental records, called your next of kin, your sister and your nieces."

Nodding along as he told me the news, I almost missed it when he said "nieces." I had this horrible visual of a mutt gnawing on my rotting arm, bone in mouth, and growling at moving object crossing his path. Even a fluttering leaf was not left unchecked. I had to take my attention away from the gluttonous pooch to remember the comment about my sister and her daughters. My sister had girls? Since when? Does she have them now? How old are they? I was so confused. I knew time was different on this side, but I didn't think so much of it had lapsed. Perhaps they had found me in the distant future? "So, nieces, you say?"

"Yes," he said as he pointed to a picture frame. "You see those girls in that picture on the mantle above the fireplace?"

"Yeah," I said, even more confused as I recognized the picture on his mantle to be the same one that I passed every morning on my nightstand. I hadn't thought much about it; to me it was like one of those pictures in the store with the stock photo in the frame. It hadn't occurred to me that it could be something more than that.

"Those are your nieces; your sister was pregnant when you were taken from us. She did not get the chance to tell you. I have been watching her raise her babies from here. They are beautiful and smart little girls. I wish I had had the opportunity to play with them on Earth, but sadly I was not given that blessing. The frame in your house—that was a gift from me. When I knew you had arrived, I made sure to have one on your nightstand for you to always see. Though you did not know who they were, it was there so that you could watch them grow. Nothing is here by accident; everything has a purpose. Every soul you meet, every item in your home, it is all here by design and necessity."

"You mean to tell me this whole time I have been staring at my own family and never knew it?" I was shocked and saddened that I had never bothered to ask, so upset with myself that I would miss such an obvious thing, something clearly set in front of my face as a reminder. Never once had I cared to pursue it.

"Don't be so hard on yourself. Clearly you had a lot going on, and something small like that is hard to see. I do not blame you one bit. I figured once everything settled down for you, you would ask. You have never been able to be the star of the show; you always took a back seat and cared more for others. This was your time to be the center of it all."

"I guess that is true, but that just brings me back to Mason. The poor kid is honestly the center of everything I have been shown. Even in my own death, I didn't even take center stage!" I laughed hysterically. I couldn't help but laugh. I had never been one to be the center of attention, just as my dad had said, and even after death I hadn't had any urge to work on myself; it was all about Mason and what happened to him and how I could help him. Though it had not been that long since I had been shown my own history, I was obsessed with this little boy whom I had fixated on needing to help. I had never once thought of myself, outside of wanting to know if my body was ever found. That was only out of curiosity, while I focused on the child.

We both went silent for a moment while I thought through a few things. I needed to sort out my own details and was still occupied by the reflection in the mirror. I contorted my face in different ways as I looked at myself on any reflective surface I could find. The coffee mug in my hand proved to be useful for this. I went so far as to toss my hair side to side. I had never been so vain in my life, and now that I liked what I saw in the mirror, it gave me more confidence. Something I found thoroughly exhilarating and surprising. I was almost fearful that if I cared too much about it, it would miraculously disappear, so I made sure to not ever look at myself for too long in the reflection in my mug.

After I had finished focusing on my looks, I thought about Mason. I still felt the pain I had felt for him the moment I saw him tackled to the ground. My concern for him still was my main motivation. Yes, I had a few other things I now wanted to look into further, but that child tugged at my heartstrings, and I needed to know. I didn't think I would be able to move on without knowing.

"Dad, I still need to know about Mason. Yes, I know it isn't part of my path and you do not know more than you have already told me, but I won't be able to get past this one. I feel like he and I are intertwined. I can't just leave him behind."

"Carol, you have to understand, you aren't leaving him behind. He is on his own path, and though you feel yours in intertwined with his, you are but a moment of sadness in his life from his point of view. I know that is hard to hear and maybe even harder to understand."

It was a devastating blow. I sat in silence, thinking about his gall in saying that to me. It took some time for me to even speak to him; it took even longer for my thoughts to make themselves coherent. I needed to leave, not out of anger but rather out of confusion. So much had happened my mind had stopped being able to process it all. I wanted so badly to know more and to fight my father on the last atrocity he had bestowed on me. Though he had been gentle in his delivery, it still stung like a hundred bee stings directly into my chest. I stood up, gave him a long hug, and headed toward the door. "I will see you soon, I promise," I told him as I made my way out the front door into the crisp, cool breeze coming off the lake.

I lingered in my steps before heading into the woods. The warmth from the sun and the breeze from the lake were soothing and helped calm my mind. I liked the wind through my hair and the warmth on my skin; they calmed my double vision and stinging chest. I swayed with each ebb and flow of the wind, listening to the song being played on the leaves and carried through the trees. I followed the breeze and lullaby as it sang to me into the woods, beckoning me to follow it home. I couldn't have fought it even if I had tried.

CHAPTER 15

Before long, I was home. I didn't need much motivation to picture my nice, warm bed, to expedite my journey. I sat on the edge of the bed, and with the picture of my nieces in hand, I watched as time flashed before my eyes. Within what felt like blinks of an eye, the little babies were transforming into little girls, and through my never-ending tears, they transformed into young women. I could not describe it as anything less than magical to behold how these girls transformed, and I was only able to view them through the small portal of a picture frame.

"They are beautiful, aren't they?" came his familiar voice. I didn't bother to even look up at him. I wouldn't be able to even make out his face until the tears died down.

I was able to manage "Yes, they are."

With a gentle stroke of his arm, he smoothed my hair off my shoulder and behind my ear. "It runs in the family," he said, barely above a whisper.

My heart started to race, bringing back memories of the conversation I had just had with my father. He was right. Of course he was; he always was. But this time, in some small way, I had hoped he was wrong. Not because I didn't want it to be true, but because I was too embarrassed to have missed all the signs. I was able to turn and face Gabe as his eyes bored into me with a strengthened intensity. I could only return their gaze for short periods and could never match his intensity.

"I see you have found yourself," he said to me.

I set the frame down on my nightstand and tried to lock into his gaze, knowing I could do so only in short bursts. "Yes, I found myself and much more," I said as I nodded toward the picture. "Did you know about this… well, of course you knew about this. You know about everything, don't you? You know everything about me."

"I try to do my research, yes. Does that upset you?"

"Well, no, of course not. How could it? I just feel like there is still so much I do not know or understand, and some of that has to do with you."

"With me?" he questioned.

"Yes, with you. Gabe, I am not one to beat around the bush. I need to know, and I need to hear it from you so that we are on the same page."

"All right. Fire away," he said calmly.

"Do you have feelings for me? More than a caretaker should?"

With a slight hesitation, he replied, "Yes. I have tried to be as professional as I could be, but I have not felt this way since Diana. Though you have not been able to see it in yourself the whole time I have known you, I saw the beautiful women sitting beside me, the woman you are now. How could I not fall in love with you? You are the only soul more concerned for others than yourself; you have asked for only minimal information about yourself and have sought to help others rather than forward your own transition. Even against my guidance, you have chosen to follow that little boy. At first I showed you his life to see how you would react—my little experiment to see how selfless you truly were. I was not to show you everything you were given, but I could not help it, especially toward the end. I was urged by the others to proceed with caution, as I was playing with fire and breaking the rules for you, but I could not help it. You were so lost and so desperately needed to know. Very much like a mother who has lost their own child to an untimely demise, you treated Mason like he was your child, and I could not bear to take that away from you. I was unable to show you more than what you had already seen, not because I didn't want to, but out of fear I would have to endure greater consequences for my actions."

Literally picking my jaw up with my hand before a fly could fly into it, I said, "Gabe, I don't even know what to say. I feel so stupid for not knowing all this, but what you are telling me is like the last pieces fitting into the puzzle. It was hard for me to see what was happening with Mason, and yet I needed to know. I had not the slightest inclination you were doing something against your own rules to give that to me. I am forever in your debt."

"Carol," he said as he touched my face with his warm, inviting hand, "I do not want you to ever feel like you owe me anything. I did this for you because—"

I felt it. I knew what he was going to say before his lips could even form the words. It was a sensation I had never felt before. I could hear my heartbeat, I could feel time slow down all around me, and I needed him in a way I had never known on Earth. "Because you love me," I finished his sentence and leaned in for his kiss.

It startled us both—the instant mental connection. I could feel his emotions and even read some of his thoughts, and as his heart quickened in pace, I could tell he felt the same way. We embraced, feeling the warmth of each other's skin, letting the other into our minds, creating what felt like an unbreakable bond. This was when we felt it, a sharp, white light cutting into Gabe like a knife. A searing pain tore us apart, and with a look of fear on his face, we both knew—he had been caught. He disappeared within the blink of an eye, leaving me behind, feeling naked, afraid, and vulnerable. "What have I done?" I shouted. I knew I had made him cross a line through our newfound connection. An action he would have to pay for. I had finally found a companion, and within moments of realizing it, I had lost him, possibly for eternity.

I threw myself onto my bed with a resurgence of tears. How could I have been so dumb? I sobbed and rocked myself to sleep. It was the only thing that could dull the pain.

CHAPTER 16

For days I heard nothing, not a single sound, not a single word spoken. As I was bathed in silence, all I could hear was my heartbeat and my tears. Gabe had been taken from me. I had only had him for an instant, and he was now gone. How could he have been so cruel, punishing a man for falling in love? He claimed to know my soul inside and out, and yet he had denied me the pleasure I was never able to find in life.

I felt doomed and insignificant. I could not stop questioning whether I would ever find happiness and fulfillment in my time. Was this his way of making me transition when I did not want to? Did he know Gabe would hold me back, and did this hinder his cruel master plan in some way? I could not get past my grief, past my hurt, and past my guilt, which was worst of all. It was my fault Gabe was being punished, my fault he was going through whatever it was he was now putting him through. My mind was reeling with the possibilities.

I could do very little with the time I spent awake. Too

upset to talk, and even too distracted to read. I read several books cover to cover, but I could not remember a single character, a single event. My mind was completely gone, and I had been left with an absentminded stare. I sat on my front porch doing just that, staring off into the distance. I sat for full days, from rising sun to setting sun, without making the slightest noise, only moving to stroke the soft fur of my ever-happy cat, who was there by my side to console me. This desolation lasted for an inestimable length of time. It felt like a day but could have been week; it was certainly a shock when I heard a noise coming from the kitchen.

In an almost complete state of panic, I jumped out of bed at the noise. It was not extremely loud. No dramatic crash or banging. Just a few shuffling noises. But since it had been so long since someone else had been in the house, it alarmed me. I leaped out of bed, sending Kiki flying off the covers; I crash-landed onto the ground. It had been such a long time since I had used my legs that I, of course, face-planted into the floor. Luckily bones did not break in heaven, so I was able to leap up unharmed, having only suffered a bruised ego and a minor tingling in my legs.

Trying to determine where the noise was coming from, I stealthily walked around the bed, being as quiet as possible, and tucked myself next to the doorframe. I wanted to get as close as possible without whoever was in my house knowing I was home. My heart was pounding with adrenaline. I was scared and curious at the same. I stood by and listened, and the shuffling continued. The person seemed to stay on the other side of the house; this calmed and confused me. "Why would they not look through the house to make sure they were alone?" I whispered to myself. This caused the shuffling to stop and my heart to skip a beat! I had given myself away! I freaked out! Midmeltdown, I saw Kiki out of the corner of my eye. She was clearly unhappy with the rude awakening and unaware of the intruder scare I was experiencing. She came sauntering out, meowing in discontent, and waltzed out of the bedroom and into the hallway. She showed not the faintest hint of fear, and not a single piece of fur was out of place. I watched helplessly as Kiki flicked her tail all the way into the kitchen, where she stopped, turned her head, meowed a slow, disheartened meow, looked back and me, and continued out through the front door. She had her own little cat door so she could come out and join me for my morning coffee. This time she used it to escape me, the little traitor.

Based on her fearless reaction to whoever was in the kitchen, I decided to be brave and called out, "Who's there?" I waited, holding my breath so as not to miss a single word or footstep.

After a minute I got my response. Walking out from in the kitchen and into the streaming daylight of the hall I could make out the distinct features of my apple-eating love. My heart leaped out of my chest, and I flew to his side—almost literally. With the force of my impact, the apple went flying across the room, and I knocked Gabe to the floor, smothering him in tears and kisses.

"Carol," he said, laughing as I continued to smother

him in kisses, and he gasped for breath. "Carol, calm yourself," he said as he eased me off him gently. He helped me to my feet from our tumble to the ground, and hand in hand we walked to the couch. We sat down facing one another with eyes locked. I did not want to blink in fear he would disappear again. This led to so many questions.

"I thought you were gone forever. I thought he would have punished you for wanting to be with me. I thought I had lost you." My voice broke on the last statement.

With his hand gently caressing mine, he said, "I thought the same thing. When he pulled me up to him, he looked at me and asked one simple question: 'What does your heart desire?' I told him the truth. My heart desired you. I didn't realize it at first, but I knew I was happier and safer with you around me, much more calm and content. Even when you annoyed me, I wanted you there. He looked at me once more and said, 'You know what will happen next, don't you? As they have done with Diana?' I said yes, and with a flash of his hand, my extensive knowledge of the rest of my charges disappeared from my memory. I fully expected you to be wiped away as well and for me to go into the human world destined to search for you until we could meet again, but I remembered everything about you and Diana."

"But how?"

"I asked him that very question. He smiled at me and told me that because I had remained devout through so many devastations and cases that would have driven any other man mad, he had given me the gift of my memories of you and Diana so that I might enjoy what it meant to love. It is a gift I am eternally grateful for. As soon as I was able, I came straight here."

With tears flowing I threw myself into his arms. The warmth I felt in his embrace was and still is like nothing I have ever felt before. One thing puzzled me. "But why did he let you keep your memories of Diana?"

A strained look came across his face as he said, "When I asked the same thing, he said I would know why when I saw her next. This leads me to believe she has strayed far from a good path, and though I am free from my duties, I am still bound to her."

Not knowing how to feel about what he had just told me, I chose to let it go and be happy. He and I could be together, a notion I had not considered until only recently and now was wholly consumed with. I was happy and in love; what could bring me more joy than this heaven? Why would anyone ever want to leave?

We spent days talking, learning everything about each other. It only took days since he knew everything about me, and it made the conversation very one-sided, actually. But it was worth it. I loved him. It was easy to love him; he made is so simple, it was almost elegant. I could laugh hysterically at him, and he never once judged me. For a brief time, it was perfection, pure bliss. Something so pure and unadulterated I could barely believe it was true.

We continued on in my little home, which was slowly becoming our little home. Things began to appear that were his, and the refrigerator was full of apples, something that always put a smile on my face. We would go for walks and spend hours in comfortable silence. As long as we were together, nothing needed to be said. I had forgotten all my troubles and was finally happy.

Time would continue forward in its usual manner, Gabe and I remaining blissfully ignorant and holed up in our happy little home. I would wake on my side of the bed as usual, and we got into a routine.

One morning I awoke to something slightly strange. This changed our happy little routine and brought the past back to haunt me.

The photo on my nightstand fell over. It was the one I fell asleep beside every night and the one I woke to with a smile on my face, knowing my beautiful nieces were growing up and becoming strong young women. I knew that much to be true, because my sister would never have allowed it to be otherwise. I woke to the picture, frame and all, lying facedown on the nightstand. I thought maybe the cat had dropped it in the middle of the night—a little strange I did not wake at the sound, but stranger things had happened. I picked up the picture and put it back on the nightstand, but the expression on my one niece's face was not what I remembered it to be.

Though she was not frowning or upset, it wasn't the usual beautiful smile. It was more like a forced, fake smile, something entirely off. I sat there with picture in hand, studying every inch of her expression, even comparing it to her sister's. I wanted to understand why it was so different than how I remembered it. Something definitely was not right.

I called out to Gabe. "Gabe, did you notice anything odd last night?"

He popped his head around the corner from the bathroom, "Odd? How so?"

"Well, my picture was lying flat on the nightstand. Did you hear it fall over in the middle of the night?"

With a pause and a slight look of concern, he said, "No. I didn't hear it fall. Is it broken? Or do they look different?"

I thought to myself, *What an odd thing to say.* His face remained unchanged as I looked at him quizzically. With hesitation, I said, "They look different—or rather, just her," I said as I pointed to one niece. "Her smile isn't quite right; what does that mean?" I asked as I handed him the picture.

He took the picture, looked at it thoroughly, and handed it back to me. "When pictures change, it is because they will age with you, but the expressions on their faces should remain the same because it is a direct reflection on their soul, what they are made up of. If they are an angry person you will see it in their expression—they will look angry throughout their life, until they come here, at which point they will disappear from the picture completely. When their expression changes, that means something traumatic, or in some cases beautiful, has happened to them, and they have changed their whole demeanor; that is how they will be from this point on."

Awestruck, I asked him to continue.

"In this case, your niece has had something traumatic happen to her. To know exactly what the event is, you will need to check into her file. But knowing what I know about your life, I know what it is that has changed her."

"Wait, you mean to tell me you know more about me than what you have already told me about? Is this about Mason or Ali? Why would you keep information from me?"

"Carol, I don't want to see you hurt, and I knew this would hurt you. I couldn't bring myself to tell you…"

"If you don't tell me right now, I will go straight to the library and look up her file to figure it out for myself!" I shouted at him. It was so unlike me to scream. I was not a screamer in life, and I even scared myself a little at this moment.

"You deserve to know." He started speaking, sorrow in his eyes. "But I think you will need to sit down. It is a little complicated."

CHAPTER 17

As I followed Gabe to the couch, my heart was pounding out of my chest. I could feel the airway constricting as I clutched my chest with my trembling hands. How could my life still cause so much pain, even after I was gone and had been gone for so long? I know my departure from Earth had not been under the greatest conditions, but life went on, seemingly happily, without me. Was that not truly the case? Looking into Gabe's eyes, I could already feel what he was going to tell me, but I needed to know for sure.

"So this is something I have only kept from you so that you would not feel the need to dwell on the past, on something you cannot change and that will cause you anguish. I knew it would come up eventually, but I had hoped it would not have the same sting if you had more time. The picture of your niece has changed because she was the one who pursued justice in the case of your death. Though she never knew you personally growing up, your mother and sister made you out to be a saint.

This is not far from the truth, so it made her search for justice all the more necessary to her existence. After you passed, your body was not found for some time. She was only a teenager when you were found. Your mother was too old to be told the news, and your sister was the one left to the task."

"It took that long to find me? How did they ever even know it was me?"

"The police pieced it all together with DNA from your sister, as well as dental records. I believe your father may have told you this already, but that was because I was the one that told him."

"But why was I not shown this? I was shown the child but not my own body being found? I don't understand…"

"Because when they found your body, they found another one with you."

My head was spinning. "Another?"

"Yes," he said with a lowered head. "They found Mason buried within a few yards of you."

I wanted so badly for the child to still be alive and well. I had hoped he had not met a gruesome demise and that he had managed an escape. I knew after seeing him tackled to the ground something was not right. I would have been shown more, but it had ended there. I needed to know, and that sole task is what drove me. I let it go, based on my own selfish pursuits. I was heart-broken and furious with myself.

"Carol, please hear the rest of what I have to say. I do not have the heart to do this to you again. You must know now, once and for all. Once your bodies were uncovered, the police had little choice but to leave it as foul play and close your files. Your niece could not take it and searched on her own to find out what happened to you, as well as to Mason. There was not a direct link between you two, and it was only by chance she was able to get the information that changed her.

"She had uncovered the two men who had grabbed him, but the connection to you was seemingly lost. A deathbed confession by Ali connected the dots. He confessed having abducted countless children. He gave the names of his contacts, but by that point they were all long gone. He spoke of the two children he had lost before they could get to their owners and the one woman he regrettably killed in the process. He had great remorse for your death, so much that he was still able to detail the experience, even though he could not recall all the details related to the countless children he had abducted."

"This doesn't make it ok! His regretting one death does not mean he was not a monster! All those children—they all went through hell on Earth. Why does that not weigh on his conscience! Why can he not see their pain!" I was hysterical. I could not help myself.

"I know it hurts—all this information. I know it is painful, but I am almost done. After he confessed, the police took all the information from the old files and closed them. This is what changed your niece—the injustice in his being able to spend his entire life free, not having to face going to jail or being executed for his crimes. Worst of it all, he thrived on the money he made in the process. She changed knowing the atrocities of his crimes and your happenstantial involvement. She became a bitter and cynical soul because of the pain he had caused your family, as well as Mason's and so many more. After Ali gave his confession, the children's families were notified, and they came forward with their unspeakable grief."

"Did he say where the families could find their babies—clearly not babies anymore—but did he give them a starting point for finding their loved ones?"

"He did not know this; he only knew the buyers and could only venture a guess as to where they went after they were purchased."

The idea was sickening. I clutched my chest and my stomach in response to the churning sensation and pain this was causing me. Not only had he ended my life and those of so many innocent children directly and indirectly, but he had also hurt another generation with his actions.

"It pains me to tell you this all, but now you know."

"Is Ali on this side now? What about Mason? I would like to see him."

With mixed emotions and hesitation, he said, "Carol, both Mason and Ali are not quite in heaven."

"What! What does that even mean? Where are they? In hell?"

"No, no, no. There is no such place. They are in a self-inflicted purgatory; that's the best way I can describe it. Ali is spending at least the beginning of his eternity fighting his own demons. He created his own hell based on his actions in life. Until he is able to work through them, he will not be able to experience heaven as we know it."

"Will he ever pull himself out of it? Will he ever be able to experience this?"

"That is hard to say. Some come out eventually; some don't come out at all. Some souls are able to be pulled out by loved ones that know they were not as horrible as they perceived themselves to be. This situation pertains in particular to extremely devout people who fear heaven and do not deem themselves worthy of it based on the slightest offense."

"I see. But why is Mason punishing himself? He did nothing wrong."

"Mason is not there as a punishment. He is there because he does not know where he is."

"Do you mean he doesn't know he died?"

"Yes. He is stuck reliving the nightmare scenario he knew on Earth because he cannot pull himself out of it. He thinks it is real, and he has created his own demons and will battle them until he realizes they are not truly there."

"The poor child must be terrified."

"He is. He may be saved by his family when they make it here to meet him; they can go after him and pull him out. Until then, Mason is lost."

Contemplating this, I said, "What if I helped him? What if I went in and pulled him out?"

"Carol, you are not his family."

"Yes, but we share a connection."

"The bond needs to be strong enough to withstand the journey; it is not an easy one. I do not recommend you do this. Please do not try; it is likely you will get stuck with him trying to fend off his demons. This is extremely risky and dark territory. You do not know what you will encounter. He died young, and his creativity gets the best of him. He can create scenarios and demons far more intense and terrifying than most aged souls could imagine. You do not know what you will find when you get there. I cannot in good faith let you do this."

With a look of complete and utter defiance, I responded, "I wasn't asking your permission." And with that I decided what I was going to do. I would go to this purgatory and free Mason from his own hell.

ABOUT THE AUTHOR

Maria Herron is the charming and sophisticated author to this debut bestselling novel. She has spent the last 5 years in the heart of the Amazon rainforest studying the mating rituals of Heliconius Butterflies and in her spare time restores Renaissance paintings.

In reality she lives in Michigan, is sarcastic to a fault, not interested in boasting and after googling that butterfly she thinks they are jerks.